This Is Not How It Was Supposed to Go

This Is Not How It Was Supposed to Go

A novel by

Tahira Chloe Mahdi

three
zero
media

© 2023 Tahira Chloe Mahdi.

Tahira Chloe Mahdi
This Is Not How It Was Supposed to Go

All rights reserved. No part of this publication may be reproduced, stored in a retrieval system or transmitted in any form or by any means, electronic, mechanical, photocopying, recording or otherwise without the prior permision of the publisher or in accordance with the provisions of the Copyright, Designs and Patents Act 1988 or under the terms of any licence permitting limited copying issued by the Copyright Licensing Agency.

Published by: ThreeZeroMedia

ThreeZeroMedia.com

Tuff Crowd Conglomerate is an imprint of ThreeZeroMedia

Text Design by: ThreeZeroMedia

Cover Design by: ThreeZeroMedia

ISBN 978-0-9740591-3-6

Distributed by: Lightning Source LLC

ingramcontent.com

Printed and bound via IngramSpark in the United States of America

I dedicate this book to my husband because he was such a huge help in bringing it to Life. He says that somewhere in an alternate universe, this stuff was actually happening, and I was channeling it. Cheeuhs, Dahling. Perfect franchise.

1

If the year 2010 couldn't bring flying cars, it should at least have ushered me into one of the six PhD programs I applied to. It took me long enough to get over the shame of waiting until 29 to go back to school. At 32, things were finally coming together for me, and now here I am. Unemployed and moving back to my mother's house. This is not how it was supposed to go.

Devastated describes this feeling well. *Depressed* is closer. *Dead inside* hits the nail on the head.

"Oh, good! I'll have some company!" was my mother's response to my need to move back home for a few months.

It also turns out that my stepfather will be away for the summer, caught between wrapping up estate/end-of-life stuff for his mother and doing something for his military or government job that will prove he's still got the juice this close to retirement.

My mother always knows when I am mentally unwell. These are the times she reminds me of the generations of Black women who had no choices and no depression because their children still had to eat, regardless of how low their moods were. Her series of supposes goes like this: "Suppose when it was time to go to the bathroom, you had to walk through the tall grass to get to the outhouse?" "Suppose you had Boo-Boo and BamBam who needed food and nobody wanted to take you in with two kids?" "Suppose you were married and had the kind of man who…"

To her, and all the other women I know her age, me being single, child-free, and college-educated means I have no problems. With "so much going for me," there is no such thing as a mood disorder. "All you need to do," they say, is find a job—shit, be a teacher, everybody loves teachers—and enjoy my freedom.

Could it be my turn, though, to take a summer off to find myself?

In every crisis there is opportunity, or something like that. I am sure I have heard that sentiment in many forms attributed to an Asian culture the speaker knew nothing about. Right now, though, it's hitting me as my self-esteem hits the pavement. I am determined to stay above the dark abyss of disappointing my mother. One thing I can't do right now is reek of laziness.

So, when my mother and I run into Junior Stave's mother at the store while we're picking up groceries for my extended stay, I say yes when she asks me to join the town's community association.

"We would love to have some young blood in the room!" schmoozes Ms. Stave. "And you'll be getting your PhD too?"

We don't tell her I didn't actually get into any programs.

"Oh, you must be so busy," she says sincerely, "but please, please consider joining us. We meet every two weeks, that's not a lot. And officials from the County come to meetings sometimes. They need somebody like you! Young people these days don't do nothing but put pictures on the Facebook."

I accept Ms. Stave's invitation because my mother is witnessing this, and she needs to see me as busy and important and smart if it kills me. I am a future Doctor of Philosophy. No resume gap here, folks. During this time, I shall be employed as a member of the Association Board for our majority-Black incorporated town. There is no pay, but I will be rich in experience.

And now you are familiar with my self-motivation speech.

♪ ♪ ♪

This Town Association Meeting is me, Ms. Stave, and eleven other people who make up the community association and town council, and then the mayor. Everyone here is a senior citizen except me and somebody's grandchild who is running around. Ms. Stave's son Junior shows up at these every-other-Wednesday meetings because they pay him a few dollars to cook food either on the grill outside the town hall or at his house—which is also his mother's house—and sell dinners to raise money.

While Ms. Margaret Stave rants about the loitering outside the liquor store, I excuse myself to see if Junior needs help. Junior Stave has been "Junior" for so long, I forget what his real name is. He was a few years ahead of me in school, so by the time I entered high school, he had already graduated. I knew him, though, because like most of the other guys in the neighborhood, he played basketball up at the park with my friend best friend Kaia's older brother Kai. Junior was cool enough and looked alright enough to get girls back in the day. He's not what anyone would call *fine*, a bit of a chubby build, probably 5'10. He has a kid somewhere but has never been married.

"Heyyy, Roshawn," he drawls when I walk up to his grill outside. Oh, I see Junior went from alright-looking to kinda cute. In a grown man manning a grill kinda way, I mean. What is he, like, 37 now? I like men who can cook.

"Heyyy, June," I answer, mimicking him. "You good? You need anything?"

"Nah, I'm good. How you been? I heard you was back."

"Yeah, just for the summer," I say, as if I know it to be true.

"Oh? What school you get into?"

Damn, how does he know I was supposed to be in grad school? I am the world's worst liar, and I am aware that my face has already fallen and given away the fact that I may indeed be here past this summer.

"Ay man, keep hope alive, you know," I answer, admitting defeat.

"I hear that. You smart as shit, though. You be back up in there soon."

I like Junior. "Thanks," I say, with the first small, genuine smile I have felt from myself in months.

"How your mother doin'?" he asks.

"She good," I say, relaxing into me and Junior being friends. "My stepfather gone for the summer, so it's 'bout to be one long ass Girls' Night over there!" I add with a chuckle.

"Aw, shit! Don't hurt nobody!" he says, turning over some boneless chicken breasts. "Come back before you leave, I'll put two dinners aside for y'all." He saw my face about to find an excuse for why I didn't have money to pay him. "Don't worry 'bout it, I got'chu."

"Ma will be so grateful. Thank you!"

"Wit' her fine self, she can have whatever she want!" He roared with laughter, designed to mess with me, but also to ensure the compliment gets back to her. "What'chu doin' after this?"

"Nothin', goin' home."

"You should come up to The Roost. They do half-price drinks every other Wednesday."

I pause to seriously consider it. Running on the same schedule as the Town Meetings, there is a place with half-price drinks? Honestly, I think I'ma need it. "Oh! Okay, then!"

"Pick you up at 9?" he asks.

"I'll be ready!" My mood has drastically improved.

Fuck. Wait. Does this mean I have a date with Junior?

♪ ♪ ♪

Junior picks me up in an older model Chevy Silverado. I had passed along his message to Ma when I brought her boxed dinner home, so she comes out on the porch to say hello.

"Hey Junior! You know how to grill some chicken, don'tchu?" she yells out to him.

He leans out of the driver's window. "Yeah, just place your order. I can send you a plate anytime you want!"

Wow. Is he trying to impress my mother already? Well, good for him. That's the respectful, polite thing to do. Especially since he ain't got no money. Better sell that personality.

"Alright! I'ma take you up on it!" She poses with one hand on her hip and one on the railing, basking in this 37-year-old's attention while I make my way up into the pickup. It's kind of adorable.

Yes, Ma. At 54, you still got it.

"I'll have her back at a decent time!" He chuckles as he pulls off. On the ten-minute drive to The Roost, he recounts the Who's Who of the town for me: who moved away, who got put away, who passed away, and who is still trying to find a way.

We walk into The Roost and there are just enough people to make a decent night out—not too many where the place feels crowded, and not too few where the place feels dead. I love places like this with a good number of tables and chairs. There's an L-shaped bar that could accommodate six seats and room to stand around, a small room off to the side with a pool table, and a DJ booth in the corner. Nothing fancy, just perfect to drink, laugh, and talk shit. Sports posters are all over the walls, so when they want to show a game on the big screen, people can feel like they came to a sports bar.

As soon as we walk up to the bar, I reach into my purse.

"I got'chu," says Junior, picking up on my hesitation.

I was right. I like Junior. He seems really effortless, like everything is chill with him all the time.

"You drinkin' with us?" He raises an eyebrow like he expects me to order a soda.

"You already know!" He don't know me at all.

"No, I mean, you drinkin' *our* drink? We got our own drink here."

"Hook me up, then!" A community *we* sounds awesome.

"How you doin' baby?" asks the bartender, a short woman in a shoulder-length blonde bob wig, wearing a black spandex romper with no bra.

"Good. Lemme get two Green Machines." They converse with each other as if they talk all the time. "Y'all win that game last week?"

Damn, this is like the tv show *Cheers* but in the hood. The vibe of the place just feels like everybody is used to one another.

I turn from the bar to look around, and a male voice shouts right up on me. "Ro-Ro!! Is that Ro-Ro?!"

It's Kai, my old best friend's big brother. "Hey Big Kai!" I exclaim, throwing my arms around his waist as he towers over me and assumes his familiar protective role.

"How long you visitin'?" he asked, looking questioningly at Junior. Back in the day, half his time was spent discouraging the older boys from talking to me and his sister Kaia.

"I'll be here a while," I say, noticing my increased acceptance of the fact that I am indeed *back home*.

"Good, come on, we over here," he says, leading me to a group sitting at two tables pushed together. "June'll bring your drink." Kai pulls my chair out for me, and I say hello to the four other guys sitting there. "Y'all know Roshawn, right? Used to be with Kaia all the time?"

They murmur "oh yeah" and "what's up" and check me out in the most polite way they can manage. When I observe the brownish-tinged green liquid they are drinking from glass tumblers, Junior comes to sit down and hands me one. Everybody still sittin' upright, so I guess the Green Machine isn't as scary as it looks. I take a sip and it's strong with streaks of almost-sweetness, but mostly just tastes like men trying to prove their manliness to one another. A few more sips, and it tastes like home.

Over the next three hours, we are joined by a couple and one other single woman. By midnight when we leave to go home, I forget all about being an unemployed, old ass college graduate who has to live with my parents.

When Junior pulls up to the house to drop me off, I don't feel like I have to worry about him trying to kiss me. The night didn't feel like a date, and our vibe felt more friendly than sexual. I'm open to thinking about it next time, though.

"Alright, thanks June," I say, reaching for the door handle before he can put the car in park.

"A'ight, I'll see you," Junior says.

Only the living room light is on, and it seems Ma is already asleep. If she were awake, she would have been in the living room watching tv and all up in my business. With two of those Green Machines in me, I was knocked out as soon as my head hit the pillow.

I wake up refreshed, though. I may not have a job, but I have a new friend. And for some reason, that gives me energy.

2

I'm feeling like one of those women in a cheesy tv movie: moving back to the small town she grew up in after having a career in the big city. You know, the ones where she opens a flower shop and falls in love with either a self-employed guy in flannel or a corporate guy in a nice suit who seemed like a dick at first but turns out to be perfect for her.

Junior could be my guy in flannel. Over the last week or so, I have been entertaining daydreams about having myself a nice little summer fling. And a fling means it doesn't matter at all that he is over 30, living with his mother (and 16-year-old daughter in Junior's case) and getting by doing odd jobs and selling dinners. One thing those cheesy tv movies always gets right is the naked capacity of *the ordinary* to be delectably sweet and thoroughly satiating.

At the next Town Meeting, I sit beside Ms. Stave, having decided to get on her good side. The whole hour and a half, I'm just a-nodding along to her points, frowning when she frowns, adding a punctuated "hmm" to conversation spaces.

The whole room perks up when she announces,

"The district's Business and Economic Development Manager confirmed his attendance at our next meeting." She continued flipping through a folder of random papers. "We can give him the information you collected, Jim, about the businesses within the town limits."

Lord, why are older people either completely disorganized and computer illiterate or way over-organized and, like, proficient in Excel?

Well, if I'ma be bangin' her son this summer, Ms. Stave may as well know I have a brain. If she is going to be seeing a lot more of me, I don't want her to think I'll also end up living in her basement.

"Will we have a report prepared for him?" I ask.

She looked at me like I'm stupid and waved the file inches from my face. "I just said we're going to tell him what we found."

"Well, in school, I was trained on how to compile reports on community engagement—specifically for elected officials. Do you all do that?" I know they don't, but it's my turn to make her feel stupid.

"You sayin' you know how to get all that into one report?" asks Jim, who put all those loose papers in the folder.

"Yep." I'm still thinking about Ms. Stave waving that file in my face, and I have changed my mind about impressing her. Fuck her.

A woman whose name I can't remember interjects, "Oh, you did say you were getting your PhD! Let's show the County we know what we're doing over here! Hand her that folder."

Ms. Stave's immediate concession to this woman reminds me that the woman is the mayor of the town.

"Can you have it ready in two weeks?" the mayor asks me.

"Yes ma'am," I assure her. I am taking the folder from Ms. Stave but snatching her soul.

"Aren't you glad I brought her on?" bragged Ms. Stave to no one in particular.

When the meeting ends, I go outside to Junior's setup, where he has already shut down the grill and is packing things away. On a self-worth high, I attempt another demonstration of my worthiness by setting the work folder down and picking up a chair to fold.

He stops what he is doing to ask, "What are you doing?"

"Just helping you out." I walk a folded chair toward the building.

He takes the chair from me. "Girl, go home."

"Damn, it's like that?" I let him take the chair from me.

He ignores my question but looks me directly in the eyes. "You comin' out tonight?" His eyes have a sadness in them but, like, a sadness that suggests he's totally willing to lose himself in sex to make it feel better for a while.

"Okay." I hold his gaze. May as well start the foreplay now. Let's get this party started. "You pickin' me up?"

"What'chu think?" He walks the chair the rest of the way to the building. I like the way the beads of sweat look on his bald head when he is walking back toward me.

I think I might fuck your sadness away, that's what.

"See you at 9." I turn and walk to my car.

♪ ♪ ♪

After my shower, I put on a cotton dress that my grandmother handmade for my mother in the 1980s. It's knee-length with three-quarter length sleeves and a pattern of large pink and white flowers on a black background. I used to think it was so country-looking, but last year, I was visiting my mother and she asked me to accompany her to some work thing. The Grandma-made 80s dress was the only thing she had that would fit me. I felt like a goofball but didn't really care enough to be embarrassed with Ma's work crowd. However, every man in the room made it a point to spend time talking to me. It wasn't until a woman in masculine clothes told me, "Girl, you are wearing that dress!" that I discovered its potential. I spent the rest of the event talking to her and contemplating the power of this old-school, ordinary thing. The skirt hangs loosely but flaunts the curve of my butt. The elastic waist cinches just right, and the top lays ever so elegantly over my D-cups, making it not so obvious that my boobs are competing with my stomach for which sits out past the other.

This should be able to lift up easily when it gets all hot and heavy in Junior's truck later. There is no way I'm bringing him to my old childhood bedroom, and I'll be damned if I get it in under Ms. Stave's roof.

I put on the black sandals that have been my go-to pair for summer dates over the past couple of years. The heel is low but high enough for me to keep my feminine energy afloat. Upon close inspection, they do look like I have been wearing them for three years, so I'ma get this last summer's worth out of them.

I hear Junior pull up, but then the loud grumble of his engine stops, indicating he has turned off the ignition. Is he coming to the door to get me? Why, Junior, you gentleman. He must feel it in the air tonight, as well. I am still selecting shades of lipstick to blend, so I let Ma get the door.

I open the door to yell, "I'll be out in a second, June!" and close it right back to finish my lipstick.

This is one of the times I wish I could do my own elaborate makeup, but my natural shade of brown is somehow impossible to match with the brands of foundation I have tried. I always end up looking like a corpse. As a male makeup artist once told me during an especially frustrating visit to the M.A.C. store, "Thank the Lord for your thick eyebrows and eyelashes. Let's just get your lipstick right." Something about my face frequently provokes heterosexual women to tell me how much better I would look in makeup and heterosexual men to congratulate me on not wearing any.

My bedroom is right around the corner from the living room, and I can usually hear conversations from either place if I'm in the other. Tonight, I can only hear low tones and chuckles from my mother and Junior making small talk. He must be trying to impress my mother like I tried to impress his. Right on schedule, my dude. Let's make this a respectable summer fling.

In the living room, Junior and my mother are sitting and talking comfortably. She is eating from a Styrofoam container—with her fingers.

"June brought me some dinner!" She makes a

point to suck the sauce off her forefinger with a loud smacking noise. "Mmm mmm!"

"Ma!" How embarrassing. "Get a fork!"

"I don't need no fork!" She picks up a potato wedge and waves it around before stuffing the whole thing in her mouth.

Junior is so amused by her unrestrained praise of his cooking. He's just grinning like he 'bout to be part of the family. Looks like I'ma have to explain the Summer Dick rules and boundaries to him. And to my mother.

"I'm ready, we can go now," I say to break their buddy-buddy spell.

They both rise reluctantly, still relishing this brief moment of my embarrassment. Junior's still smiling as we walk to the car. When he pulls off and honks the horn, she is standing on the porch waving goodbye with a whole turkey wing.

"Your mom cool as shit."

Little does he know. "Mm hmm. Crazy is the word."

"Your stepfather seems more serious."

I shrug. "She claims opposites attract."

"They must be pretty stable, bein' able to be apart for months at a time." He sounds like he admires that about them. That sadness from his eyes I now hear in his voice.

"I guess. I never saw what she sees in him," I admit. But I need to switch gears right quick. "What's your first name?"

"How you don't know my name?" He whips his head around to glare at me.

"Eyes on the road!"

He looks forward again and shakes his head. "Mm mm mm."

"We weren't even in school together!" I'm just proud of myself for wanting to know his name before I see his penis.

Instead of answering me, he turns up his sound system. Tupac? Really?

Oh, well. Some dudes need motorcycles and some need facial hair, but me not knowing Junior's name will make him more exciting for now.

The parking lot at The Roost has a lot more cars this time. The inside is not uncomfortably packed, but there may be only two empty seats in the place. People are also standing near the bar or along the walls. Once again, we head straight for the bar.

"You want the Green?" he teases, in a better mood since walking in.

"You know what, let me start slow with my usual. Gimme a Amaretto with ice." If I am contemplating taking my panties off in a pickup truck, a slow seduction of my own senses will be better for the whole experience.

"That's it?" he sneers.

And just like last time, someone we know comes up to us, yelling my name.

"Ro!" It's Gene, another guy from Kai's old crew. He is my age and goofball-tall. Like, there is basketball-tall, model-tall, gets-girls-because-he's-tall, and goofball-tall. No one ever wondered why Gene didn't play professional basketball, only why he would never keep a job. He was supposed to graduate with me and

Kaia but didn't make it. And he wasn't one of the ones who didn't make it because he got locked up or shot. He just…didn't make it.

"You comin' to the cookout?" Gene takes a gulp from his Green Machine.

"What cookout?"

"This Saturday, up at the park. We doin' a big Father's Day thing."

Gene doesn't have kids. But since he never works except the few times he's selling smalltime weed for someone in his family, he is always on hand to help out when the fathers are coaching on the sidelines of their kids' football games, when someone is moving, and other times they need extra hands.

"Oh, I'll try to make it." *Who am I kidding? I can't wait to hit my first hood cookout of the summer.*

"Yeah, I told your mom earlier," says Junior.

That same bartender walks over. Her wig is pink-red and shorter this time and not as laid as the blonde one. Junior leans in and engages her in conversation. *I'm not jealous. It's whatever. Just get my drink.*

"You lookin' healthy, babygirl," Gene exclaims, putting his arm around me and leading me to the table where all the guys in their crew are sitting. Funny how everybody just knows Junior will bring my drink along later. *A lady could get used to this.*

I thank one of the guys for getting up to give me his seat, but he is on his way to talk to a woman on the other side of the room. The men are in the middle of a conversation, and because the music is loud, there is no whispering. I don't think they care, though.

"June still fuckin' Mimi?" One of them asks, his

eyes darting quickly to me and then back to the bar. I am not sure whether that statement was because he was genuinely curious or because he wanted to give me food for thought.

Nobody else looked my way, and most were looking into their cell phones or around the room as if they were surveying the scene. Their eyes all went to the bar for a few seconds, watching Junior shoot the breeze with the bartender. I take it her name is Mimi.

"Nah, he squashed that a long time ago," confirms Gene. "Since her baby fahva got out."

"They still fuckin'," the guy scoffed, turning his attention to his phone.

I didn't take into account that I've lived away from my old neighborhood for almost twelve years. I can't possibly know who's been smashing who as I roll through town on a summertime dick mission. Anyway, it's only a competition. And there's one thing this overachiever is good at: competition. Sex is the easiest thing in life I have ever gotten, but in this case, I want to be the *only* summertime boo.

Junior is walking over with my drink when he answers his phone. He hands me my Amaretto and keeps talking and walking to the door. Good old Gene keeps making small talk and jokes with me while I sit here and pretend I don't care that I gotta compete with Wiggy Mimi. I don't wanna compete with Wiggy Mimi. I'm sad, he's sad, we can cheer each other up and then get on with our lives. It can be that easy.

I look around to see what other men this bar has to offer. Junior is not the only game in town. Why am I acting like the Summer Dick has to be his?

Gene exclaims another name. "Dinko!"

I turn to look at the guy walking toward us.

I am immediately struck. Stricken. Strook.

I think my heart stopped. He is at least six feet tall. Not too slim, coming off almost muscular, and his shoulders are broad enough for me to imagine my legs up on them. Neat, thick dreadlocks that aren't too neat but just right, not quite shoulder-length, but heavy with some swing to 'em. I can taste his brown skin from here, like somebody has figured out the secret to the perfect cup of black tea with honey. Damn. Bright but very easy smile, and those eyelashes, God almighty. Is that a little stud nose ring? Oh Lord, my stomach flipped. How is this person just walking the streets looking this good? I need to look away.

He daps all the brothers sitting around us. He pauses at me as if he was about to give me dap but thought better of it.

"That's Roshawn," says Gene. "She from around the way."

He gives me a backwards nod. "Wha'sup." He sits down right across from me, and I can smell him. Cocoa butter scented lotion on his skin, an oil from a familiar hair care brand in his locks. He turns away from me to talk to one of the guys. Thank God. Now I can breathe.

I'm gonna need another drink, NOW. Where is Junior? My gaze slides from the bar to the door. When I look back at the people I'm sitting with, that one guy who warned me about Junior is just glancing away from me back to his phone. Shit, what's more embarrassing, the thought of him catching me thunderstruck by this Dinko person or him catching me looking for Junior?

I have about $300 in my bank account. I can buy myself a drink. Let's let this little country dress do its job up in here.

I stand and gently pull the skirt of my dress out from me in case it was sticking to the backs of my legs. My underwear confirms that Dinko caused a biological reaction too. Must be the drink. I am walking to the bar and I can feel his presence behind me and it is a lot to be going through right now.

I order another Amaretto and ice directly from Wiggy Mimi who doesn't seem like she is registering me as a threat or competition or anything but another customer.

Gene comes to my rescue again at the bar. "Ro, you smoke?"

"I do tonight," I blurted. That's the Amaretto. Without even making me feel drunk, it just takes all the inhibition away. And now I am suddenly self-conscious about my walk as I make my way back to the table.

He is still there, smelling good and smiling easy. I don't know with to do with myself, so I just sip and look around. Next thing I know, here comes Junior.

"Silas, Gene," Junior motions toward the door. "Help me get Pete in the car. That fool threw up outside."

Junior seems to have asked the biggest of the guys to help him out. Several other guys also stand up, including Dinko. We all follow Junior outside. I casually hold my drink down by my side so no one will peep me walking out the door with it.

That one who threw me the Mimi warning is named Silas. He stands up and lands at about 6'2 with that kind of thick build that is average for men these days. His resting face makes me think he's the type who has always had an old soul. With his close-cropped, thick, curly hair, he kinda looks like if the rapper Slim Thug were a congressman. He's wearing a button-up shirt as if that's just his thing—to wear a nice shirt to a bar.

The parking lot has its own little party, complete with a thumping bass from somebody's ride. People are sitting in and on cars, lounging and having their smokes. As we watch Junior, Gene, and Silas put a big dude in the front seat of Junior's truck, Dinko lights a cigarette. Standing right beside me.

I am going to fucking melt right into the fucking ground.

Can he feel me feeling him? I am doing all kinds of telepathy. I am making mental pictures of us orgasming together and sending them directly into his mind.

Junior and Gene walk over to us and light cigarettes. Silas goes back inside. I sip my drink, knowing that the drunk guy in the passenger seat is not the only reason I won't be exchanging sexual comforts with Junior tonight.

Junior who? I want whatever this Dinko is dealing.

The men chat for a few minutes as my summertime fling plans change. "A'ight, Ro, lemme get'chu home," Junior sighs.

Cockblocked for the second time in a matter of minutes.

Gene walks toward the passenger side of a nearby car. He has never driven a car or gotten his license, to my knowledge.

Junior puts his cigarette out in a receptacle. "You can sit in the back and we'll drop Pete off first." He walks toward his truck without looking at me. A sadness looms about him.

"Good night," I say to Dinko without looking at him, though I let my hips talk to him as I walk away.

When Junior drops me off, his mind is elsewhere. He doesn't seem any more interested in sex with me than I am in sex with him. We say good night and I get in the house, empty glass from the bar still in my hand. I am so mad that I wasted two Amarettos and this dress—and that I came so close to trying to smash Junior Stave.

However, the invention of things that go bzzz in the night means that I have a quick outlet for my frustration, and all I have to do is think of the first time I laid eyes on Dinko.

3

Ma didn't want to go to the Father's Day picnic. She said she wasn't interested in trying to be sociable with Margaret Stave and her bunch. She also can't imagine adults having a good time with a bunch of children running around. Her reasons for not going damn near kept me from going, but it's 5:00pm and I'm craving cookout food and social possibilities. If they have been at the park since 2:00 and will be shutting down when it starts to get dark, I can roll through in time to get a plate, grab a drink, and get in on an afterparty.

    I have waited all day to shower so I can be as fresh as possible. I oil up my legs and arms with Avon's Skin So Soft, and apply my fruit-scented shea butter on my torso and back. The temperature that shows up on my phone says 90 degrees, so it's really not my fault that I have to break out my shortest cutoff jean shorts. There's nowhere else I would ever wear these but to a cookout in a park on a really hot day. With canvas loafers and an off-the-shoulder t-shirt bearing my college logo, my outfit is just right for a couple of hours at the park. Thank God I went back to a perm; my hair is finally past my chin, so I can pull it back neatly enough with a headband.

The park is close enough that I would feel dumb driving there. As soon as I get a good stride down the street, here come Ms. Stave driving up from the direction of the park.

She rolls down the window of her Jaguar. "You late, ain'tchu?"

"Yeah, I had a bunch of stuff to do today. My mom said to tell you hello and she's sorry she missed catching up with you." Ma ain't say all that, but I knew that would make her go away.

"OK, then. I can't wait to see that report." She waves and drives on.

The air encompassing the park is sweet and comforting with the aromas of charcoal smoke, meat, and scented sweat. I ate two honey buns before I left the house so I wouldn't appear as if I were counting on this picked-over food for dinner. The food has to be lukewarm by now, but a hamburger and some cheese curls will do me just fine. I see Junior right away and wave to him but keep my distance. There is some other woman standing with him, talking.

"Get over here, Roshawn!" my old friend Kaia shouts. I run to her as she runs to me and we almost knock my plate to the ground as we hug. "How's the graduate?"

"Ugh, girl," I groan. "You don't wanna know."

"I *do* wanna know. You deleted your Facebook page?"

"Yeah, girl, the same day I put my stuff in storage. Find me a drink and I'll tell you all about it."

She directs me to sit in a section of chairs where

some other women around our age are sitting. These are the most women my own age I have been around since I've been home.

She calls to Kai to bring me a drink. He comes over with a tropical flavored wine cooler. It's a start. I tell Kaia all about my fall from grace and hype up my search for employment until I can apply to grad school again.

"I am proud of you, sister." Kaia probably knows me better than anyone, and I didn't realize how much her encouragement would mean to me right now. "It just wasn't the right time, or the right schools. Do not give up. You can do this, Smartypants." I wish I saw her more often, but she has a husband and kids and a career now. Just looking at her beautiful, tired face, I am reminded of how different our lives are.

Three of the other women in this circle are married to men who are here. Their kids run up on them every so often. These married mothers are better than most I encounter at cookouts and parties. It took me years to recognize and avoid the type of hatin' ass mothers who get very friendly and chatty with me, coerce me into conversation with their toddlers, and then sneak off and leave me to babysit so they can go feel like a person for a while.

The other two women, Nikki and Sharmel, are single with no kids and are either currently having sex with men who are here, or used to be, or both. We bond over a shared sense of freedom, like we each got 99 problems but a family ain't one. They invite me to ride with them to the afterparty at a club in the city.

Nikki looks like she would be okay-looking

if something bitter weren't eating at her core. She is missing the light that allows a person's personality and demeanor to add to their attractiveness. It's like she is made of stone and her extra pounds don't sit well. Standing at about 5'8 in her flat sandals, she comes off like a linebacker. Her skin looks smoked up and she has a permanent look of not giving a fuck.

Sharmel is short, round, and soft. She's Care Bear cute, and her demeanor is more carefree than fuckless. Her hair is cut short-short and either naturally curly or texturized just right. Her presence is peaceful, and she is the kind you can just be goofy with.

I'm finishing up my second cooler when I hear Nikki talking in a low voice to one of the married women. "I'm just tired of fuckin' this nigga," she complains. Damn, I wonder who she is talking about. The married woman laughs.

"Ay Ro, we got that if you want it," Gene offers, walking by.

I look at the rest of the women questioningly to see if they budge. They don't.

Nikki looks over to two side-by-side picnic tables off in the distance where Gene is headed. "I'm done wit' Dinko ass." She pulls her sunglasses down and picks up her phone.

Did she just say Dinko? Not Dinko and her? *Her?* She lyin'. He's so full of light and so handsome, and she is the pit of fucking despair. I mean, how? No, it may be just a lie. Hey, until I know for sure, I don't know at all.

I get up and follow Gene. People are sitting at and on the tables, and each table is circulating a blunt.

A woman at one table is rolling another. I sit down and someone puts me right in the rotation. It's the medicine I needed. We all exhale and talk about everything under the sun it seems.

Then, the sun is going down and someone is laughing about zodiac signs. Dinko says he is a Pisces. Just my luck. A Pisces man is a blessing and a curse.

"I'm a Scorpio," I volunteer, looking up at him standing there, mentally imploring him to fathom a Pisces-by-Scorpio triple-X-plosive opportunity for mountain-moving, mind-blowing freedom of sexual expression high up on a cloud of carefree in a galaxy far, far away.

He looked at me, and his eyes confirmed receipt of my message.

"Scorpio? Oh Lord, you crazy," a girl says. We all laugh and me and Dinko break our eye contact.

I stretch my legs out in front of me. The very tops of my thighs and my uterus cannot take this.

The smokers notice everyone else packing up to go, so we get up too. They are discussing plans for the club tonight. If Dinko is going to end up being my summer fling, can I really accept a ride with Nikki?

"Who you ridin' wit', Gene?" My plan is to stick close to Gene.

"I'm ridin' wit' Kai," Gene answers. "He got the most room."

I start walking toward Kai to ask if I can ride with him, but Nikki and Sharmel meet me right before I reach him. "We'll see y'all down there," Nikki calls out to Kai, communicating that *we* are me, her, and Sharmel.

Trapped. They won't pay for my drinks or for me to get into the club.

Once Nikki pulls out of the parking lot, I take another chance to break free. "I don't have any cash on me to get in," I call from the backseat, high enough to not care about looking broke.

"Girl, we ain't goin' in," Sharmel laughs. She pulls out a half-full bottle of Patrón and a sleeve of small cups from under the passenger seat. Without even asking me if I want some, she pours a little more than a shot's worth into a cup and hands it to me.

It takes about 25 minutes to get to the club in the city, and then we park. I don't know what it is about the ritual of making a party out of the cars parked outside of a club that is more fun to me than being inside the club. We get out and lean up against the hood of her red Nissan Altima, enjoying some time flirting and being flirted with.

When our neighborhood guys roll by in Kai's Yukon, I wave and blow kisses, but Nikki gives them the finger. Kai parks further down the street where we can still see them and they can see us. After Kai, Gene, Junior, and Dinko get out of the truck, they open the trunk and a skinny guy hops out. I recognize him from The Roost because he is wearing the same blue fisherman hat. He is younger than us—twenty something—and I remember the guys teasing him for trying to sell them mixtapes in his quest to be a rapper.

I watch as our guys get into the same flirting games, and Sharmel is studying them just as hard as I am. I'm looking for clues in how Junior and Dinko interact with each other. They are more interested in the women walking and riding by than they are in conversing with each other.

I hope they ain't best friends or cousins or some shit.

Nikki has been talking to and smoking with a guy from the car beside us for at least an hour. Neither Sharmel nor I have exchanged numbers or in-depth conversations with any male passersby.

"Let's go up there with Kai an'em." Sharmel is thinking what I'm thinking.

"Okay." I look over at Nikki.

"She good," Sharmel assures me. "We can ride back with the guys."

I picture us all climbing into Kai's big ass truck and I want to call 'Dinko!' the way someone would call 'Shotgun!'

The guys seem glad to have us join them, and not at all surprised that we want to ride back with them. We clown around and I am in such a happy place. I am not thinking about being a failure or broke or jobless or without my own place or unsure of my future. I feel at home with them in a way that I don't when I'm around those people who are expecting me to be an impressive enough person to secure an important position in society.

♪♪♪

Dinko has passed out in the large trunk space, and we take pictures of him before we get ready to go. It's clear that Sharmel likes the young'un, whom they call Bond (his actual name is James Bond), and they hurry to sit next to each other in the backseat. I get my wish because I'm the only other person who could fit in the trunk space with Dinko.

They wake Dinko so he can sit up, pull his knees up, and rest his head on the side back window. Kai shuts the trunk as soon as I climb in, leaving it up to me to figure out how to maneuver a comfortable position. Kai turns up the music before he pulls off, choosing a local R&B oldies station playing slow songs. The best I can do here is to mimic Dinko's position and enjoy my body touching his—if only for a cramped ride home in the back of an SUV. I let my right arm slip between his raised knees so that my hand can rest comfortably behind his shoes. His head is turned to his left, leaning against the back seat, and his right arm rests on his stomach. Once I hear Junior snoring in the backseat, his head resting to the side, I close my eyes, think about how nice the night was, and pray that we all get home safely.

After we ride a while, I hear the opening notes of "Reasons" by Earth, Wind & Fire on the radio. It's a perfect song for the perfect night that ends with me so close to Dinko. I catch myself dozing off when I feel a light brushing of my skin outside the crotch of my shorts. My knees are also up, so my situation down below must be exposed. I don't dare open my eyes, but I wonder if Dinko's hand has gotten lost. ♪ *I'm in the wrong place to be real.* The same way my hand rests behind his shoes, his hand could rest behind my shoes, but with his longer arms, his hand reaches further back, directly to the bullseye I have been mentally inviting him to. I feel my vagina spasm because he is most definitely touching me. If I am dreaming, please, don't nobody wake me up. His fingertips lightly brush against the hairs on the exposed flesh that has obviously escaped from the right side of the crotch of my shorts. This would be embarrassing, but it's obviously working to my advantage.

His fingertips keep lightly grazing and I am losing my fucking mind. ♪ *Please let me love you with all my might.* If he goes any further to the left, he will feel how wet he has me. Please, please, just move to the left. Torture and ecstasy and I just want to move my hips but I can't. His fingers move slightly to the left. Still too far away, but it's right here ... please ... ♪ *I'm longing to love you for one night.* I feel the vehicle make familiar turns, letting me know that I will likely be the first one dropped off. Why does Kai have to drop me off first? Dinko's forefinger and middle finger are no longer grazing, and they feel like they know they are running out of time and must make a decision on whether to go in. ♪ *And in the morning when I rise, no longer feeling hypnotized* ... They make it to the edge and linger, pressing gently in contemplation. His fingertips have got to be wet. We are on my street, I can tell. I feel his middle finger make a bold move to the left and touch the very threshold of this fountain just when Kai puts the car in park. Dinko pulls his hand back quickly as Junior turns around to ask, "Ro, you awake?"

4

On Sunday morning, I wake up still feeling hypnotized. The excitement of the *almost* has turned me inside out and my nose is wide open. In an effort to calm my nerves, I take my time making a breakfast of stuffed French toast with strawberries, scrambled eggs with cheddar cheese, and turkey sausage.

Ma comes into the kitchen as I am making our plates and gives me a strange look. "You was hungry, huh?" she asks, taking her plate.

"Yes, I am hungry." I really, really am. I start eating before my butt hits the dining room chair.

"Mm hmm, you was out with Junior Stave last night, huh?" She still on some Junior Stave.

"Junior, Kai, Gene, all of 'em."

"Where y'all go?" She sits down to eat.

"Some club. We didn't go in, though."

"So what'chall do?"

"Just rode around and parked outside like everybody else." I guess it sounds weird when you say it like that. "What did YOU do last night?"

"Went up to the Post." She and her friends love going to some old clubhouse for veterans. They get free drinks and flirt with old men.

"You have fun?"

"Yep." She keeps eating without offering any detail.

"I am looking for a job." Guilt breaks my spell.

"Okay." She looks at me as if that's out of left field. "Did I ask you about a job?"

"No, but…"

"Did I ask you for rent money?"

"No."

"Did I say you need to find your own food?"

"No."

"Did I say you need to marry Junior Stave so I don't have to have another mouth to feed?"

"Eww, Ma!"

"Alright, then." She scrapes cream cheese off the French toast onto her plate. "Why you put all this damn cheese on here?"

♪ ♪ ♪

I did an internet search on how to format a community engagement report and took about eight hours total over the course of several days to get it polished and professional-looking. I also waited until after 4pm on each of the days to start the work so that Ma would see me working when she came home from work.

Now it's Friday afternoon, and I am bored. My report is finished, and I'm bouncing between lonely misery and excited lust. In my head, I keep replaying my five minutes in heaven with Dinko and catching myself randomly singing aloud, *"Can't fiiind the reeason-nns ..."*

This is excruciating. I can't ask anybody for his number. Right? That would be wrong, right? I'm showing up to The Roost with Junior but asking around for Dinko's number? I deleted my damn Facebook page. That would have been the easiest thing ever, to link through someone else's page and slide in them DMs. And then there's the Nikki thing. She said she was done with him, but that doesn't mean it will look right if I play the Clean Up Woman. She went off with some guy the other night, and Dinko didn't pay her no attention, but do I want to be in the middle of all that?

If I get lonely enough, I can call or text one of the guys who have provided my sexual maintenance services in the past year or so. However, they feel strikingly different from the neighborhood guys I have come to love in these last three weeks. I'm trying to have a butt-nekkid, carefree romance without conversations that eventually get around to school, job, or career.

I decide to text Junior.

```
Me: *Sigh* What to do on a Friday night...
Junior: Want some ice cream?
```

Welp. That was easy.

I'm past trying to look cute for Junior, but I make an effort in case we run into anyone we know. A tank top, jeans, and my lil' basic black sandals will do. And lipstick. I choose a deep red color that the commercial said will last through eating and making out. I cannot believe I'm so ready to burst from more than a week of unshakeable arousal that I actually want Junior to want to kiss me after watching me seduce an ice cream cone.

As soon as I hear my mother's car's sound system blasting Stephanie Mills as she rolls up on the parking pad, I hear Junior honk the horn as he pulls up. When I walk out, my mom is getting out of her car, wearing her business casual Friday work clothes, and carrying a six-pack of Corona. I leave the door open for her.

"Oh, I see you!" Junior calls out to her. "You like Corona?"

"Yeah, I like Corona!" she boasted. "All I need is some lime!"

"You want us to get'chu some now?" Junior is doing way too much. Settle the fuck down, dude.

"Nah, y'all go ahead." She laughs. "This will be gone by then!"

"Ma, stop scaring Junior," I gripe, walking past her around to his passenger side.

The front passenger door opens from the inside and a teenage girl hops out, giggling.

"I got my daughter with me," Junior explains to Ma, who is on the porch now, instead of to me as I get in the truck.

The girl, still giggling, opens the back door and hops back in.

I look back and there are two teenage girls in the backseat. "Hellooo," I greet carefully.

"Hi," they giggle, looking at one of their phones, my presence barely making a difference.

"You want some ice cream?" he yells up to Ma. "We goin' to get some."

He still brown-nosin'. Give it up already.

"Yeah! Bring me some ice cream!" Ma looks like that's the best idea she has heard all day. Really? She can't just say 'no thank you' and let me have a date to myself? "I don't even care what kind!" she adds.

Junior is so satisfied to have a way to impress my mother that it is a complete turnoff. And here I done put on red lipstick.

We drive to Jolley's, a place situated by a waterfront with two restaurants, a dock for small boats, and an outside stage for when musicians set up to play blues or jazz. The girls get out of the truck and go off by themselves. By the time we get up to the order window for the small hut that is Jolley's Treats, I've changed my mind about tantalizing him with my cone-licking skills. I order a banana split with the works and he gets an Oreo milkshake. We sit at square table under an umbrella.

I ask about what it's like to have a 16-year-old daughter these days, and the floodgates open. According to Junior, it is not easy. She moved in with him and Ms. Stave the same weekend I moved back home. Her mother got frustrated with her and was hoping Junior could provide something she could not, especially since he is usually at home. He is only recently unemployed, having been laid off from an HVAC company a few months ago. When his father died almost 20 years ago, his mother began treating him as "the man of the house" with an unstated expectation that he lives there for as long as she is alive. His daughter, Quiana, does not like living there, so he tries to do daddy-daughter stuff to keep them both sane.

"Well, at least she has friends," I offer, nodding in

the direction of the pier where the two girls were taking pictures of wildlife in the water.

"That's her girlfriend," he says, looking over at them. "Like, *girlfriend*-girlfriend."

"Ouch," I empathized. "You okay?"

"Hey, at least I ain't gotta worry 'bout her gettin' pregnant," he chuckled. "Her mother caught them together and…" He pauses, shakes his head, and reaches for his milkshake.

"Damn." There's not much I can say. "You're a good father."

"I hope so." He slurps the last of his milkshake through his straw making a loud noise.

"Let's go mess with the teenagers." I smile at him like we have a secret between us.

The four of us have a nice evening out by the water. Junior and I relax into the girls' silliness and have a good time walking around, people watching, and taking pictures.

On the way back, Junior stops at a convenience store and comes out with a pint of Neapolitan ice cream in a thin plastic bag. He hands it to me without a word and drives five more minutes to my house.

I still don't remember his real name, but I know I'll find out soon enough. I feel a deeper bond with him now. Whether we find ourselves together romantically or not, he feels like he will always be in my life.

In contrast, I don't care if I never know Dinko's real name. All the better to be able to get the hell away from him when the fire goes out. *When all the reasons start to fade.*

5

The council loves my Community Engagement Report and are singing my praises. Several of them remark that I should use this to get a job with the County or maybe someone's political campaign—even Ms. Stave.

Once my ego is thoroughly boosted, the mayor checks her watch and murmurs about the time that this BED Manager is expected. I'm doing a search for county jobs on my phone when the room livens up. "Mr. Mercer! Good to see you!"

I look up, and Silas is walking into the room. Silas from The Roost. Silas who wanted me to know (or believe) that Junior was (still) smashing Mimi the bartender. He is wearing a nice button up shirt, khakis, and brown dressy-casual shoes.

Okay, I see you, Silas Mercer.

He looks surprised to see me but doesn't make a big deal out of it. Here, his vibe is slightly different than it is around the neighborhood guys. I mean, I know you're supposed to code switch between work and hood, but I really like the way he commands their attention and respect, resting easy in what they are treating as an important role.

After we all introduce ourselves, the mayor and the guy named Jim do most of the talking, directing him to look at different parts of my report. The meeting goes well, and the senior citizens are very pleased at the end.

"Thank you for this report." Silas nods his approval as he rises from his seat to leave. "This makes my job a lot easier. I wish everybody made it this easy."

"That was Miss Bell!" Several people say my name and smile proudly at me.

"You did this?" Silas asks me.

I'm suddenly modest, nodding with a slight smile.

He doesn't hide his admiration. "Well, shoot. Nice work."

"Thanks." I'm probably blushing.

"Make sure you tell him you need a job," adds Ms. Stave. She didn't say it snidely, but it still stings.

I am about to give her a look, but one or two other people chime in like, "Oh yeah, we need people like her," and "She's about to get her PhD, you know."

I glance him a quick look that says, *Old folks, am I right?*

"My business cards are in my car," Silas offers.

"Go get her one," orders Ms. Stave, devoid of shame. She looks at me pointedly.

Silas walks out, but I take my time putting papers in my bag before leaving the Council still chit-chatting. When I get outside, Silas is standing at Junior's grill talking and putting mustard on a smoked sausage he holds in a bun.

"You need a job?" Silas calls out to me.

I walk over to him and hope I don't look as embarrassed as I feel. "Yeah, just something to hold me over for about a year. I'm applying to graduate programs." This is the second time Silas is catching me looking pathetic. First about Junior and Mimi, now about a job. I wonder what he thinks of me.

Silas nods and takes a big bite. Junior hasn't looked at me, and I detect a few things being slammed as he cleans up.

"How's Quiana?" I ask, which feels safer than asking him how he is doing.

"She a'ight." He still doesn't look at me. "I'ma stay home tonight to keep an eye on her." He throws some things in a box and scoffs. "Fuckin' teenagers, man."

"Shit, that used to be us," Silas said, stuffing the last of the sausage into his mouth. What was that, three bites and an inhale? He dusts the crumbs from his hands. "Oh, lemme get you my card." He walks to his car.

Junior glances up at him walking away and it just doesn't look … friendly.

"Your mother tryna get him to find me a job," I explain.

"Hmph," is his reply. He keeps cleaning without engaging me in conversation.

"Say hi to Quiana for me." I guess I'll leave him alone, then.

"A'ight." He won't even look at me.

"See you later." I walk away. It doesn't seem like a good time to get into what's wrong. I stop at the driver's door of Silas' Lexus. He is sitting in the driver's seat and appears to be fishing around for cards. "Thanks a lot," I say. "I appreciate the help."

He hands a card out the window. "You goin' up to The Roost?"

"Ummm ..." I think for a second. Without Junior to drive me and buy me drinks, I don't feel like spending the money.

"You wanna get somethin' to eat?" he offers.

Well, since Junior didn't offer me no free dinner, "Okay, sure."

"Follow me."

I am in my Honda Accord coupe and driving before I process this with myself.

Eh, it's just food. Junior looked mad, though. *Junior always mad.* Is he, though? *I would like to go out to eat. I am grown.* This is not going to look good. I'm going to come off as a floozy. *Sheeit, all the floozies are gettin' some. I'm not.* Silas may be trying to give me some. *Well, he has a job, a nice car, and County district's worth of respect. Maybe this is who I should be getting closer to.* I like Dinko, though. *I can't even find Dinko, though.*

He has me following him for a half a damn hour to a fancy-ish restaurant. Lord, I didn't need all this. I could have had a beef sausage by Junior. Ha. That sounds funny. Anyway, I can tell he is impressed with himself by taking me here. He makes it a point to be a perfect gentleman about everything, and he is still playing his Important Man of County Government role.

"You drink beer?" he asks, looking over the menu.

"I want a beer."

"Yeah, depends on what kind." Takes me to this fancy place and we drinkin' beer?

"Two Modelos," he says to the waiter, who was already walking away by the time I noticed he was there.

"You ever had Modelo?"

"No."

"You'll like it. You ain't just gonna order a salad are you? You want some crab legs? Let's get crab legs."

"Okay." I like crab legs, but I am annoyed. He just picked out my food and drink for me. I can tell he's trying to be some kind of hero, but I know how to choose what I eat and drink.

He places the order and talks to me about my work with the Town Council. He then tells me all about his job as I work my way through this strange ass beer. His father had a business that did contract work with the County, so he got his job based on those connections. He explained to me his philosophy about how this is the way the world really works, and that it's all about working your connections. When our food comes, he asks if I know how to crack crab legs, and when I say that I do, he still proceeds to mansplain.

I would have ordered something that I could eat with a fork, but here we are.

"You datin' Junior?" His question comes out of nowhere, but totally from somewhere.

"No," I hesitate. "We friends. We hang out."

"I asked him, and he said y'all were friends." He hasn't broken eye contact with me and is holding a crab leg. "But whenever that dude say a woman is his friend, she always turn out to be more than that."

And how is this your business, sir? "Okay," is all I say. My face must show what I am thinking.

He adds, "I'm just asking. So I'll know if he'll get mad about me taking you out."

What the hell is going on here?

"I don't see why he would," I reply. Oh, God. This is a date?

"Good. You too good for him anyway."

I give him a disapproving look.

"I could tell when I first saw you at The Roost that you didn't belong with nobody like Junior. Or any of these other guys around here who ain't doin' nothin'. You about to get another degree too? What's Junior gonna offer somebody like you?"

"I'm not dating Junior."

"Good." He motions to the waiter to bring the check. "What'chu doin' Saturday? There's a campaign kick-off that you should go to. I'ma start introducing you to people so it'll be easier to get you a job."

And the magic word is *job*.

"Cool. I'm sure I can make it."

"What's your number?" He pulls out two phones and puts my number in both.

When the check comes, he pulls a lot of cash from a clip and silently counts out the total and tip. I purposefully picked up my phone and answered a text instead of watching him count the money.

When we get up to leave, he puts his hand on my lower back to usher me toward the door. Really, nigga?

♪ ♪ ♪

It's midnight and I am still awake. I am searching cable channels that show old movies because the black-and-white format puts me to sleep. My phone chimes with an incoming text.

Unfamiliar number: You awake?

This number is not in my phone. I'll be damned if I'm playing games this late with someone who turns out to be a person whose number I have deleted on purpose. Then again, I edited most of those contact names to come up as Asshole, FuckYouBitch, or Do Not Answer.

Unfamiliar number: This is Silas.

Here we muhfuckin go.

Me: Oh. Hello.

I save his number in my phone.

Silas: What are you doing?
Me: Trying to go to sleep.
Silas: Oh, my bad. You want me to let you go?
Me: Nah, it's ok. But if I suddenly don't text back, I am knocked out.
Silas: Good. Because I don't want to let you go.

Sigh.

Me: Why are you up?
Silas: I'm always up.
Me: That's not healthy.
Silas: You gonna help me be healthier?

> Me: How would I do that?
> Silas: By caring about my well-being.
> Me: LOL. Sure
> Silas: Why is that funny?
> Me: Because it is.
> Silas: Can you do me a favor?

Fuck. If this dude tries to get text sex, I swear, I'm going to tell Junior.

> Me: It depends...
> Silas: Of course. And I am only asking because I can't stop thinking about it.

Shit, maybe I *could* have some text sex. Junior's going through something, and I don't know how to find Dinko. Silas texts in complete sentences with proper punctuation.

Fuck it. I'm in.

> Me: What can I do for you?
> Silas: Can you wear that dress on Saturday? The one you wore to The Roost the last time?

Oh. My. Gawwwd.

> Me: Wow. Ok.
> Silas: Is that an 'ok' as in yes, you will?
> Me: Sure, I can do that.
> Silas: Thank you. Ok, I can sleep now.

```
Me: *facepalm*
Silas: Good night.
Me: Good night.
```

♪♪♪

I have gotten in the habit of having dinner cooking by the time my mother gets home from work. She made such a big deal the first time I did it about how great it was to come home and smell food cooking that now I watch cooking shows during the day for ideas. It's the least I can do to make myself useful.

She gets home between 4:55 and 5:15, depending on traffic. At 5:10, I open the front door and lean on the frame. The faint breeze coming through the screen makes me think it would be nice to put a chair out front and sit on the porch sometimes.

Good grief. This neighborhood is getting to me. I'm turning into the sit-outside type.

This time, I hear Teddy Pendergrass blaring through Ma's car system as she comes down the street. She must be thinking about my father. Growing up, she always played old music and told me stories about her and my father and his favorite artists and who they saw perform live in concert. She pulls up on the parking pad and I wave smugly. She's going to love these beef empanadas.

As she is getting out, Junior's truck rolls slowly to a stop in front of our house. Oh, Lord. What does he want? He parks but leaves it running.

She turns around. "Hey there, June!"

"Hey Miss Marshawn!" He is all smiles getting

out of the truck and looks like he's feeling better. "I brought you something." He reaches back into the truck and pulls out a six-pack of Corona.

He couldn't see me roll my eyes because he was too busy grinning up in my mother's face. Must we continue with this? I guess he's trying to put himself back in the running?

"Oh, aren't you a sweetie pie?" She takes the six-pack from him like he just unexpectedly paid her light bill.

"I was at the store and I saw the six-packs and I thought of you." Junior is sheepish and cute.

"Well, thank you! I appreciate it!" She turns to look at me and holds up the six-pack, smiling.

"What's up, June?" I am not smiling. "What'chu bring me?"

"Ask your mother if you can have a beer!" he laughs. "A'ight, I ain't gon' hold y'all. Just wanted to bring you somethin'."

I guess I gotta respect his old school approach, but he is trying too hard now.

"Alright, June! Thanks again, hear?" She waves and he honks the horn as he drives away. "Ain't that somethin?" she marvels as she steps inside the house. "Junior brought me a six-pack!"

"I see," I scoffed. "I guess he thinks this is going to help his case. It won't." I shut the door behind her.

She laughs. "Shoot, you can let him keep bringing me six-packs!"

"You know what? I sure will! You wanna take me out, bring my mother a six-pack." I sit down at the dining room table. "Dinner will be ready soon."

"Junior's nice." She sits down after tossing her purse to the side.

"I don't even know Junior's real name. He's such a *Junior*."

"Foster Stave, Jr.," Ma says.

"Foster? How you know that?"

"Because I knew Foster Stave, Senior."

"What? For real?"

"Mm hmm," she continues. "I used to leave early enough for work in the morning to get me a coffee from the convenience store. Foster was with the other men who used to go there for coffee and park off to the side and stand around. After he saw me a couple of times, he started coming in and paying for my coffee."

"WHAT?"

"Mm hmm." She takes out a beer. "Can you bring me a bottle opener?"

I get up and get her a bottle opener. "Sooo…" I sit back down, not knowing what to ask next.

"And then," she continues, popping the cap off the bottle, "one time—it was right around Thanksgiving—he started up a conversation." She takes a swig from the bottle. "And then asked me what I was making for Thanksgiving dinner. I told him, 'The usual, same thing everybody else havin'.' The man pulled out a 50-dollar bill and handed it to me." She takes a long drink.

"WHAT?"

"Mm hmm. Talkin' 'bout, 'I just wanna contribute somethin'. Hope you have a blessed holiday.'" She cracks up laughing at her own imitation of his deep voice.

"WHAT?" This is nuts. "So, Junior got it honest?"
"He got it honest." She shakes her head.
"Can I have a beer?"
"Sure."

Over dinner, Ma and I talk about men and stuff. She was under the impression that Junior took me out after the last Town Council meeting. I told her how he was acting that day, that I'm not really interested in him, how Silas Mercer emerged as a could-be contender, and that I would be going to the campaign kickoff on Saturday.

"Silas Mercer?" she ponders.

"Yeah. He used to live around here, I heard."

"Wait a minute, Silas Mercer with the four kids and the wife he's always leaving?"

"The WHO and the WHAT?!" I exclaim.

"His father owned a HVAC business, right?" She seems sure.

"His father owned some kind of business …"

"That had a contract with the County," we both say at the same time.

"Oh my God!" I exclaim. "And you think this is him? With a wife and kids?"

"Ain't too many people named Silas."

I am obviously speechless, but I still can't close my mouth.

"Ask him," she says.

"Ugh. Why would he …" I begin. I sigh and shake my head. "Never mind." I switch gears so her mind doesn't travel far down the road of me being the object of a married man's affections. "Well, he told me to come to this thing on Saturday so he can help me find a job. The mayor and Ms. Stave asked him directly to help me out."

"Well," Mom says. "Ask him about the wife and children."

♪♪♪

It's Saturday, and I started getting ready three hours before time to leave. I take time to groom my eyebrows, exfoliate, and use a little battery-powered device to get the excess fuzz off my face. I put on eyeshadow, but upon second thought, I rub most of it right back off. I need a job, not a date. I put some respectable curls in my hair, and I do put on my Grandma-made 80s dress as requested. Instead of my basic black sandals, I put on sandals with the backs closed in and a higher heel. I'm still conveying accidentally sexy, but professional.

When I arrive at the campaign event, there is a lot of standing around at tall-top tables. Most of these people seem to know one another and be really into the networking thing. The candidate is some short guy who can't seem to not talk like a politician in regular conversation. I bet he watches President Obama's speeches and practices in the mirror.

I got myself a small plate of fruit just to have something to do with my hands while I wait for Silas to show up. In the meantime, people (men) keep coming up to me at my table and asking me what I do. I have perfected shaking a man's hand and saying, "I'm representing the Town Council," while looking him in the eyes and mentally sending him a picture of us enjoying sex with each other.

I have collected nine business cards by the time I spot Silas working the room. He is wearing a very nice suit, looking handsome and exuding a casual confidence in this atmosphere. I look around, and he is the best-looking man of the four or five in his age group. He catches me watching him and motions for me to join him and the woman he is talking to. He introduces me both as representing my Town Council and as a graduate student studying social policy. I am impressed with how much he talks me up without me having to do much talking about myself.

He introduces me to at least 10 people as he makes his way around, telling people, "Give her your card. We need more young people engaged in government. I'm making sure she stays with the right people." This, he makes quick work of in a matter of seconds, then moves onto his own agenda. I mostly just stand there smiling and nodding.

Two hours later, the politician has given his speech, I have a purse full of cards, my feet hurt, and I am ready to go. I can't find Silas, and I'm glad I can just slip out. I'm tired of listening to these people talk.

I am out the door of the place, foot at the curb, almost scot-free, when I hear Silas behind me.

"You just gon' leave, huh?" He calls out, walking toward me.

I stop and turn around. "I couldn't find you. I know you got people to talk to. I'm okay."

"You got somethin' you need to do now?" His eyes are sparkling, but his face remains serious. I feel a little tingle at the base of my spine. Shit.

A black BMW X5 pulls up to the curb. The window rolls down and a brother in the passenger seat says, "Y'all ridin' with us?"

"Come on," he says to me, walking to the back door of the car and opening it for me.

I get in and adjust my dress under me. He shuts that door and walks around to the other side to get in. While we ride, the men—all County employees, I gather—talk about the event we just left and gossip about some of the people there. I ride and look out the window. Are these more people that could give me a job? Probably. I'll keep doing what I've been doing all day, smiling and nodding, speaking when I am spoken to.

We end up at the same spot where I got ice cream with Junior and company at Jolley's. Of the two waterfront restaurants there, the men lead the way to the most upscale one, and seem to know the staff pretty well when we go in. Silas is still being a gentleman and pulls out my chair for me when we sit down. They discuss appetizers, and again, no one asks me what I want. When the server comes, they order loaded potato skins, honey lemon pepper wings, calamari, cheesy flatbread, oysters from the raw bar, and four Johnnie Walkers.

These other men are older, but not too old. I put Silas at around 37 or 38 if he grew up with Junior and them. The two men with us, whom he calls Mark and Jones, look more late 40s or early 50s. After the Johnnie Walkers come, I feel more relaxed and I ease into conversation with them.

One of them mentions his wife and that reminds me to look down at Silas' left hand. There is a band on his ring finger. How did I miss that before? Something about sitting and drinking and eating with men who are all married puts me at ease, though. All I have to do is be impressive enough to get a job, and that is one thing I know I can do.

The server brings the oysters out first.

"You eat oysters?" Jones challenges me.

"Not really," I admit. Oysters are gross. Like snot in a shell.

"You allergic?" asks Silas.

"No, I've just never had them." I don't want to make a big deal out of this.

But they do. "Oh, nahhh!" and "Whaaat?!" They throw their hands up and look at me like I said I've never had chicken wings or something.

"You eatin' 'em today!" Silas announces, as Jones gets into explaining hot sauce and horseradish and this and that.

I conform to the group. Silas dresses mine for me and makes a joke about swallowing. He hands it to me, then picks his up, and the four of us throw them back at the same time.

UGH.

"Yeahhh," Jones congratulates. "What'chu think?"

I just give him a look and make a dramatic motion of finishing my drink.

"For real? You don't like it?" He is laughing, and I'm not sure if this is a thing where they all know that oysters are nasty but eat them to prove something. This reminds me of the guys drinking their Green Machines at The Roost.

"There's eight of 'em, so you gotta eat one more to keep it even," Jones proclaims, and they all agree.

"Fuck it," I say, "load it up."

They roar with laughter and Silas does me up another one. We all throw them back. Silas looks at me with happy approval.

"I need another drink," I assert.

"Oh, you *gettin'* another drink!" laughs Jones. "Fuh sho!"

The rest of the food comes, and we talk about regular stuff like music and movies. I have a good time with them. When we're finished and full, they split the check without even looking at me.

On the ride back to our cars, we laugh and talk boisterously. I feel like I have made two new friends by the time Jones lets the three of us out. As we walk to our cars, Silas walks at a slow pace with me, putting on his suit jacket. Mark reaches his car and pulls off before we make it to mine.

"I don't think I should let you drive home after two drinks," Silas says when I reach my car.

"I'm okay," I insist.

"You wanna come up?" He gently turns me around to face him.

"Come up where?" I look up at him, confused.

"Upstairs." He puts his hands in his pants pockets.

Something makes me glance at the building where the event was held. It's a fucking hotel.

"Silas." I put my hand on my hip. "Really?"

"I'm stayin' here anyway. I'm not asking you to do anything, just come up 'til you're sober enough to drive."

His face, his height, his suit, his voice, and the way he is looking at me has brought that tingle back to the base of my spine. The earlier sparkle in his eye has deepened into a projected vision of him fucking the shit out of me.

And oops, I almost forgot. I grab his left hand from his pocket and hold it up.

He takes off the wedding band and puts it in his pocket. "Not everything is what it seems," he says.

"Are you married?" I ask.

"Yeah, but ... not for long."

"Well, it just don't look right. Like, what the hell am I supposed to do?" It'd be just my luck, I fuck him tonight and find Dinko next week.

"I hear you." He steps forward, still staring into my eyes.

I back up a half-step into my car door, feeling a percolating and throbbing that is outside of my control, driven into feverish agitation with a breeze that blows across the side of my neck. *Et tu*, wind? I put my hands behind my back so my palms can grip the car in case my knees betray me and buckle.

His hands are back in his pockets as he steps forward again, landing lightly up against me. He sighs. "This dress is fuckin' killin' me."

My heart skips a beat as an anaconda alerts me to its presence in his pants.

"Fuck," I groan, turning away to look at something else. Anything else.

"You can get home ok?" he asks softly.

"Yep." I refuse to look at him.

"You sure?" He places his hands on the lower part of my hips.

My head swivels back. "Silas."

He backs up and is looking into my eyes as he

takes off his jacket. I don't want to look down, but I can't help it, I have to. I catch a glimpse of something big before he folds his jacket to hold in front of him to hide it. He reaches past me to open my car door. "Good night." His smirk says he knows I got an eyeful.

"Good night." I get into my car and am so frazzled that it takes me a second to remember that I am supposed to start the car before putting it in gear. I take a deep breath and say a prayer for my safe travel home.

6

My mother, Marshawn, didn't always live in this town. She's a big-city girl—heart and soul, down to the bone. She grew up in a major city in the next state over, about three hours from here. Her first argument with her parents was about whether she would go to an out-of-state HBCU or a PWI for college. Her parents won, and she ended up at a PWI very close to home, on her way to becoming a "big-time lawyer," as she was known to put it. She majored in political science and did very well, utilizing tokenized positions and opportunities to her advantage. She was always well-liked by everyone, and her success was due to her determination to work hard at anything that would keep her away from home.

Home was complicated. Marshawn's mother was a housewife, but also a talented seamstress who could make anything that anyone gave her a picture of. My grandmother didn't even have to bring in her own money, as there was a lot of it flowing in from my grandfather's businesses. Paul, my grandfather, just wanted her to do whatever she wanted to do.

Marshawn has a brother, Marcel, who is a few years older. He got the hell out of there as soon as he turned 18. He was gay and moved to New York with a friend and never looked back. He and Marshawn see each other when they can, but I've noticed that years go by between those times.

Granddaddy Paul's businesses were illegal dealings, but they were plentiful and successful, and he was able to keep his family safe. Or so he thought. Because of the types of "businesses" he was into, Marshawn's father had to keep a small, tight social circle. There weren't a lot of people coming around, so as Marshawn grew up, she could name all of her parents' friends and the few family members who came to parties, holidays, and barbecues. But, while Paul was busy protecting his family from trouble outside that circle, the trouble turned out to be within it.

Marshawn was 17 when her father's friend Roman started giving her money and buying her gifts. When she went to college, she was about 20 miles away and stayed on campus, feeling lonely at the PWI with no real friends. Roman would pick her up from campus from time to time and take her out to eat, to shows, and wherever she wanted to go. He was a good-looking man and could have had any woman his own age. But he wanted Marshawn.

Roman and Marshawn dated exclusively from her sophomore year of college until she graduated. With their sneaking around, most of their dates were out of town, and only a few times a month.

Marshawn graduated and got a summer internship at a law firm. She told her parents that she needed a year off before going to law school, figuring she would take that time to find a way to confess, explain, and legitimize her relationship with Roman. She worked one month in the internship before she missed her period and found out that she was pregnant with Roman's baby.

Roman had a younger sister, Zelda, who bore the horrible burden of being the first one told about Roman and Marshawn's situation. When they asked her how to break the news to their small circle, of which she was also a part, she revealed her own secret. She was having an affair with Paul and felt that they were in love. The three of them reasoned that if Zelda broke the news, Paul would not—could not—fully blow up to the point of violence.

She was wrong. Paul enlisted two other men to help him find and kill Roman. Roman took Marshawn to the next state over (where we live now) and put her up in a house to be safe while things settled down. Roman sent Zelda along to keep her company and gave Marshawn all the money he had. Roman wanted to face Paul, man to man, and let him know that he planned to marry Marshawn and take care of her and their baby. Unfortunately, when Roman came back to the city, Paul and his accomplices were all about shooting first and thinking about Marshawn and the baby later. Roman was also armed, however, and defended himself when they attacked him, firing back at the men who were firing at him. Roman and Paul were both killed by gunfire.

Marshawn's relationship with her mother has been strained since then. They do their best, but one big blow up in which Grandma accused her of getting Paul killed was enough to affect every subsequent conversation they had. I haven't see my grandmother at all in many years, but I see my Aunt Zelda, whom I call Auntie Zee, all the time. She tells me every time she sees me how much I look like my father. She and my mom are as close as sisters, and she is the extent of my extended family. On holidays, I visit Auntie Zee instead of coming back home.

My mother married Thomas when I was 20, after all those years of showing very little interest in dating. When I got to high school and she finally took a full-time job as a compliance officer, she had a "friend" here and there, but nothing serious. And then, all of a sudden, Thomas is moving into the house my father provided for us. That was my cue to leave. At least she used some of the money my father left to help me get on my feet with an apartment in Atlanta.

Thomas is dry and serious. He likes westerns and eats lima beans by themselves. Let Ma tell it, she says, "God knows what I need," instead of a reason that makes sense like, "I love him." She doesn't love him, and I know it. With him away for the summer, we can catch up on some extended quality time. Something is still broken between us, though, like an invisible wedge that keeps us from being as close as we could be.

7

At 10am on the Fourth of July, I am finishing a 'party-size' bag of Doritos, feeling like my thoughts, emotions, and general sense of self is off. I feel like a foreigner in my own head and body because something in me has passed the threshold of *Fuck it*.

See, if I had a job with benefits, I could get a therapist. Until then, it's self-medication, and today is the perfect day to find some. While I'm contemplating which park would have the best cookout crowd I can blend into, I hear my text alert.

It's Silas. My heart races.

> Silas: What are you up to today?
> Me: Trying to get into something. What are you up to?
> Silas: Having a pool party. You are invited.
> Me: Really? Where?
> Silas: My father's house. I will send the address. It's an adult pool party.

If he is attempting to get me alone, he picked the right day for an indecent proposal.

    Me: Adult??
    Silas: NO KIDS. Adults only. Open bar, food, and a DJ. Bring a friend if you want. My father knows too many dudes. Not enough women.
    Me: LOL, I can bring my mom for the old dudes.
    Silas: Perfect. Just come through. We will fire up the grill around 3.

He sends the address and I text my mother instead of yelling upstairs.

    Me: We have been invited to an adult pool party.
    Marshawn: Adult? People are going to be naked or something?
    Me: HAHAHAHAHAHAHAHAHAHAHAHAHA

It takes her 10 minutes to come down to the living room.

"Who is having an adult pool party?" she demands.

I crack up laughing before answering. "Silas Mercer says they are having a pool party at his father's house. No kids."

"A pool party?" She frowns. "Them old ass men make me sick. All they want is to see some skin. I bet they all gon' have on t-shirts and jeans."

"Oh, you want to see them in some swimming trunks?" I joked.

"Hell no. But I wouldn't show them no skin either."

"You wanna go? He said open bar and a DJ."

"They gonna have food?" She got the nerve to be hesitating like she don't wanna go.

"Yep, he said 'food.'"

"What'chu wearin'?" Miss Marshawn is in there like swimwear.

♪ ♪ ♪

Jason Mercer has a large, beautiful home, built for parties and entertaining. We drive up and park head-in along a wooden fence with about 20 other cars. The music is set at a comfortably loud volume, and we can tell by Harold Melvin & the Blue Notes that the old heads are running this shindig. An opening in the fence leads to a pathway that winds past the side of the house around to the backyard. For people to enter the front of the house, they would have to keep driving past where we parked and follow the road around to the driveway and garage on the opposite side.

I have only seen a backyard like this on tv. There is an outside kitchen, a gazebo, the inground rectangular pool, a pergola, and plenty of lawn space for chairs and tables. County contract money must be good.

Silas greets us immediately and leads us over to meet his father. Jason looks just like Silas but shorter, with a nice shiny bald head, and he looks less arrogant than I expected him to. Jason shows enough class to politely shake our hands and welcome us, then wait until Ma's back is turned to glance down at her butt and give Silas an appreciative look.

She is wearing a one-piece hot pink bathing suit, denim shorts, and a black coverup that looks like a net. I have on an electric blue two-piece that only lets the slightest band of skin show above the high-waisted bottoms, with a long, flowy, sheer coverup that fits like a maxi dress.

We take our time to audibly gush over what Jason has done with the place to give ourselves a moment to choose our post-up spot. There are five or six couples who look to be in their 50s and 60s sitting together in chairs under the pergola or in lawn chairs with umbrellas by the pool. A few men and two women are hanging around in the bar and kitchen area. Reading each other's minds, we head for two unoccupied, isolated chairs with an umbrella between them. It's close to the bar, near the DJ, but we won't have to talk to anyone unless they come to us.

As soon as we settle in, the two women by the bar walk over to their respective men and start unnecessary conversations. Ma and I exchange a look, knowing that the women just want to make sure we know which ones are off-limits.

About 10 more people arrive, and the DJ is really starting to feel himself. With his head full of gray hair, big smile, bedazzled t-shirt, and banner with his name on it, he looks like a lot of fun. "Greetings, everybody," he booms into the microphone. "I'm DJ Willie Pea. Y'all can be shy all you want, but I'ma get'chu dancin! Somebody bring these ladies over here a drink." He is talking about us.

Silas walks up to us. "Y'all want a drink?"

"I want a drink!" Marshawn wants a drink but will make me get up to get it. She looks at me and I get up.

I don't know how to be around Silas now. I feel like everyone can tell by watching us interact that we are a few drinks away from being more than friends. Will a drink or two or three help me relax enough to get over it or relax enough to get *into* it?

Silas walks me to the bar and introduces me to Benny the Bartender, a man with a relaxer in his slicked-back hair, a hoop earring in his left ear, and a smarmy grin. He offers to make me something special and I tell him to make two. Benny holds me in conversation while he takes his time making the drinks. Silas talks to the other men by the bar.

Right when Benny is telling me the story of how he once made a drink for Oran "Juice" Jones, Silas suddenly turns his attention to us. "A'ight, man, damn, you over here tryna romance an' shit!" He tried to sound playful, but it comes off very jealous.

Benny grins, flattered that Silas regards him as a rival. "Here you go, darlin'." He hands me two Tequila Sunrises.

"Thank you," I say sweetly, taking a drink in each hand. Benny has zero chance with me, but how dare Silas, with his married ass. I walk the drinks back to my mother and see more people walking into the backyard.

Here come Junior, Gene, Bond, Sharmel, and... I cannot breathe... Dinko. My knees fail me, but I make it gracefully into my chair.

"Man, I told you to bring some women!" Silas hollers.

Junior and company walk right up to me and my mother. "But my women right here, though," smirks Junior. "Wha'sup, ladies? Glad to see y'all here."

Silas actually looks mad. He walks away to give his attention to the nearby food setup.

Without missing a beat, Junior instructs Gene and Bond to find some chairs and bring them over here so they can all sit with us. Gene and Bond bring four chairs and then head straight to the bar with Dinko and Sharmel.

Junior plops down and commences to fawning in my mother's face. Jeez, Junior, have some dignity.

Silas announces that the food is ready and party guests are making their way over to check out the spread.

"I'll get'chu a plate, Miss Marshawn," offers Junior, standing up. "You don't have to get up."

"Why, thank you, June!" She is doing a very good job of holding in a laugh as Junior beats everyone to the food.

"Nigga, let the women get the food first!" Silas mistakes Junior's pandering for greed.

"Nigga, I'm gettin Miss Marshawn a plate!" Junior protests.

"Ro, come get a plate!" Silas calls to me.

"I'm okay for now," I lie.

Dinko's arrival necessitates an emergency adjustment to my initial pool party plan to just sit here drinking and eating. I'm hungry as shit, but I'll be damned if I sit here eating burgers, chicken, and potato salad before I show him some skin while my gut is at its lowest point of the day. My plan now is to get up enough alcohol-fueled courage to take off this coverup and get in the pool. He has me so hot that I am looking forward to submerging my body in that water to cool the fuck down.

    As this area fills with people, I glance over at the bar. Dinko has just gotten his drink and is sitting on a barstool, facing away from the bar. He has one heel on the stool's footrest and one foot on the ground and this positioning is doing something to me. The light blue of his swim shorts is the perfect color on him. The length and thickness of his legs makes me fantasize about him standing up while I bounce on his dick. He has on a dark blue tank top, and even though he doesn't have the most chiseled muscles, his upper body, chest, arms, all of it looks strong and solid. Damn, that's a well-made man. He has fashioned a white t-shirt into a turban halo crown, letting some of his locs fall out in the back. I am picturing myself wrapped around him and he looks directly at me. This whole backyard disappears for a second and my world is just Dinko sipping his drink, holding my gaze. Fuck. Me. I am so embarrassed that I don't know whether to smile or play it off, so I just look away and bite my bottom lip as hard as I can. The pain helps me fight off the sexual stimulation.

    I drink my cocktail in about three gulps. Lemme go holler at my man Benny for another one.

    "You drivin', remember," my mother cautions as I get up and head that way.

    Why the fuck did I bring her? I could be offering Dinko several types of rides later tonight. I ignore her and walk to the bar as Junior arrives with her plate.

Benny is happy to have me back. "You want another one?" He steady grinnin'.

"I need a stronger one this time, Benny." Thank God there's an open stool at the end of the bar. It only accommodates five stools, and this is the furthest away I can get from the blaze of a thousand suns that is Dinko. I will not look at him, but I want to be near him. Benny will keep me company while I escape my mother's nagging and nurse my drink.

"Where your phone at?" Silas sidles up to me holding a plate. He is keeping his voice at a low tone.

"In my bag." I turn to look over to my abandoned seat. Dinko is walking over to our group of friends who are sitting there eating and laughing with my mother.

"I been textin' you."

"What the texts say?" I challenge.

He looks at me like he knows I am giving him the blues. "I made the devilled eggs. You wanna try one?" He holds out the plate.

I guess I should feed this alcohol. Passing out drunk would be too much time away from Dinko. I eat three, listening to him tell me about food and his father's famous grilled mac n cheese and how most people don't know the right way to smoke meat.

Our friends over there are getting really loud with their laughing and I can tell he feels just as left out as I do. We both instinctively get up and walk over to them.

"Ol' Feel-Em-Up Foster!" Gene hollers. He and everyone else nearly falls out their chairs with laughter.

"What are y'all doing?" I ask, sitting down to get

away from Silas.

Gene is the only one who can stop laughing long enough to answer me. "Did you know Junior was goin' to massage school?"

I look at Junior and he is shaking his head in only mild embarrassment. "Since when?" I ask.

"I start the day after tomorrow." He looks proud of himself despite the fun being made of him.

"That's nice!" I am happy for him. I know he's been having a rough time. "That's good money you can make with your own business!"

"That's what I said," Marshawn chimes. "In this day and age, you need as many skills and hustles as you can get!"

"Tickle-Me Foster!" Bond howls.

Silas slips away and tends to his hosting duties. DJ Willie Pea plays on, and the sun gets a little lower in the sky.

When Junior gets up to go to the bathroom, the rest of the young(er) folks head for the pool. It's just me and my mother again.

"Junior's gon' take me home," she says. "He gon' take you home too when y'all are finished partying." I disregard the lecture in her tone because this is the greatest possible development.

"You ready to go?" I ask, feigning concern.

"Yeah, that's enough o' this." She grabs her purse from under her chair. "Your phone has been going off."

I look at my phone. Silas has been texting me the whole time I've been here.

```
Silas: I can tell you don't even know how
       beautiful you look.
Silas: So, do I get to make you a plate?
Silas: Are you getting in the pool?
Silas: Try my devilled eggs, at least.
```

I want to ask where the wife is and what about the kids I've heard about. But Dinko is over there looking good in the pool, and I don't give a shit about what Silas has going on.

"So who's the one with the dreadlocks?" Marshawn inquires, looking toward the pool.

I take a deep breath, "That," and exhale, "is Dinko."

"Dinko?" she sneers, making a face.

I shrug as if to say, *I didn't choose his name*.

"Mm hmm. Tomorrow, you gon' tell me you like Dinko."

My mouth falls open and my heads spins to face her.

"You been starin' at him all day," she says, as if I have been *that* obvious.

Damn, have I been *that* obvious?

Then, Junior is back from the bathroom, Dinko is up out of the pool, and DJ Willie Pea is showing off.

"By special request," DJ Willie Pea croons into the mic.

The backyard erupts as Lenny Williams pours out his heart and soul. Everybody here is singing along to "'Cause I Love You." Junior is sitting back with his eyes closed singing, Gene is on his knees singing, Bond is holding Sharmel close in the pool singing, and Dinko is walking up, dripping wet, singing. The whole party is bonding with every *"Oh Oh Oh"* we shout together. My phone buzzes in my hand.

> `Silas:` `Now you know we should be slow`
> `       grinding off this one.`

I smirk, knowing that wherever he is, he is watching my reaction.

Dinko sits down beside me. "You stayin', right?"

I look at him to answer and my stomach drops like I'm on a rollercoaster. I say, "Yep," and look away quickly.

Silas walks up. "You want somethin' else to eat?"

Cockblocking with his own cock. Brilliant move. I'm tipsy enough to actually enjoy having Dinko beside me and Silas standing in front of me.

"Probably, after I get in the pool. You got devilled eggs left?" It's been a while since I have had two dudes demonstrating interest in me at the same time, in the same place. My ego needs this, to be honest.

"Nope. Told you to get some more," Silas fusses. "It's some mac 'n cheese left. And some burgers."

"Can you put some to the side for me? I didn't want to be too full to swim." I feel like I have the upper hand, so I am going to use it for whatever it's worth.

He goes off to fulfill my request, looking only slightly defeated.

Meanwhile, Marshawn can't wait to get out of here, and Junior can't wait to prove how responsible he is. They leave and I am free to increase my intoxication.

"You can swim?" asks Dinko.

"Nah, I just wanna get wet." I was mid-sentence before I heard how it sounded, but I didn't blush about it.

Dinko hoots a big, "Ha ha haaaaaa!" as he stands up. He drags out a blushing, "Woooo ..."

"I'ma get another drink, then I'm gettin in the pool." I stand up and head for the bar. Fortunately, Benny is talking to another woman, so I only get a wink with whatever drink he hands to me. Since most of the people using the pool are using the closest to the house, I walk all the way around to the opposite side before sitting on the edge to let my legs dangle in the water.

As the sun goes down, DJ Willie Pea continues with classic slow songs. A few other couples besides Sharmel and Bond get in and out of the pool to slow dance.

Dinko has already climbed back in. "What'chu waitin' for?" And now he is coming toward me.

I slip in, not even grimacing at the chill, finding my footing where the water barely reaches my shoulders. A familiar song starts, and the party exclaims appreciation.

"Don't let Bootsy write you a check yo' ass can't cash," says DJ Willie Pea into the mic.

Dinko reaches me and I wrap my arms around him.

"Ay! Don'tchall leave no fluids in my pool!" shouts Jason Mercer.

The party guests find that hilarious and start cracking their own jokes about the couples slow dancing in the water.

His hands start off on my waist. But to get the

rhythm we need, he has to hold me closer and sway me from side to side. The song is strumming every nerve in my body. ♪ *I'd rather be with you-hoo, yeah.* His hands move across my back, slide to my hips, and then around to my lower back. It's like he is trying to memorize the feel of my curves. I slip my hands from the tops of his shoulders to his upper arms. With my fingertips, I trace his triceps up to his shoulders and pause for few beats before reaching up the back of his neck into the locs at the base of his skull. ♪ *I wanna be your number one, so get to that.* I gently grab two hands full of his hair and turn my face upward as he bends his head to rest his forehead on mine. I can't feel that thang yet, but his body feels so good pressed up against me. He is so firm and thick. We keep this steady, sensuous groove to the point where we were both breathing heavily. ♪ *If I can't have you to myself, then life's no fun.* He hasn't even moved his hands down to grip what I know he wants to grip, and I can't place his hands there because my fingertips are sliding rhythmically across his shoulder blades. Our mouths are close enough to feel, smell, and damn near taste each other's breath, but I feel the agreement between us that we can't kiss right now. We absolutely cannot. Not right now. But that just makes me want him even more. Is the water around us boiling because oh my gaawwdd …

The next song was halfway over when Jason yelled, "Last call for alcohol!"

We both took the cue and voluntarily detached our soul bond to come back to reality.

"Yeah, you a problem," he muttered.

"Me?"

We laugh and pull away from each other. Sharmel is giving me the *'Girrrrl!'* face from over Bond's shoulder, and we make our way toward each other in the middle of the pool.

"Somebody havin' fun," Sharmel teases.

"Yup, just some fun," I giggle, intoxicated. "I'm hungry now."

"Ay, come get your plate." Silas is rather solemn, standing at the edge of the pool looking down at me.

Welp. Fuck it. I wish Junior had seen too. We can narrow this down right now. Anyway, I am feeling my drinks and don't care. But I am hungry, so I wade to the steps and up out of the pool.

Silas is holding my coverup. He holds it out for me to step into and puts his hand on my back to lead me into the kitchen inside the house.

"You can sit down," he says, putting a plate in the microwave to heat it.

I sit at the island in the large kitchen that looks like it's out of some fancy architectural magazine. "This is a nice kitchen."

"You know Dinko mess wit' Nikki, right?" he says, leaning back on the counter.

"I know he *used* to."

"Who told you that?" His brow is furrowed like it's not the truth.

"I heard Nikki say it."

"Don't let that dude lie to you," he warns. He takes the plate from the microwave and sets it in front of me. "I let his ass know I was watchin' him so he couldn't try anything."

Silas was right there watching me freak Dinko in

the pool? I'm glad I'm drunk. Anyway, this smoked mac 'n cheese and the hotdog with no bun is hittin.

Silas never sits down; he leans right back on the counter and goes into his phone. As soon as my plate is nearly done, he walks outside and comes back in with my bag—and with Kai.

"Hey!" I garble with my mouth full. I knew someone was missing from the party.

"Wha'sup, young'un," Kai greets. "You ready?"
I'm confused.

"Come on," comforts Kai. "I'm takin' you home." He helps me off the stool and Silas hands him my bag.

"I'm not THAT drunk, dag!" I protest.

"You still can't drive. Come on." Kai puts his arm around me to lead me out.

"I can't stay 'til the party is over?"

"It's over!" the men say in unison.

Well, damn.

8

Junior takes me back to my car the next morning. He's brooding again and quiet on the ride to Silas' father's house.

"You ready to start your classes?" The least I can do is try to cheer him up.

He sighs. "I'm ready. I won't be doin' the dinners for a while, the Town Meetin' dinners. Class is Monday, Wednesday, and Friday nights."

"Aww, damn! So what they gon' do?"

"Gene gon' take over."

"That's good for him."

Junior scoffs. "Yeah, if he can stay consistent. He just be…" He stops and shakes his head.

"He's no Junior Stave," I chuckle.

"Ay, if Silas ask you out, say no." Junior looks at me. "You heard me?"

"Why you think he would ask me out?"

"Man, I ain't stupid," he answers, offended.

Shit. Silas warned me about Junior and Dinko, and now Junior is warning me about Silas. The evidence keeps piling up to inform me that my crushes are not as secret as I want them to be. Especially not when they all know each other.

"Silas is married," I say, as if that fact has had any degree of impact on Silas' interactions with me.

"Even beyond that. He can be shady as shit."

We reach Jason Mercer's house and Silas is standing at the side of it, where he can see us pull up. Junior gets out when I do, and all three of us give a quick raise of chins and hands for a greeting.

Junior waits for me to get in my car before he gets back into his truck. Then, he follows me all the way home, waits for me to get in the house, and pulls off without a word or honk. I don't see my mother's car, so she must have gone out.

My phone chimes with a text as soon as I walk in the door. I don't have to look at it to know that it's from Silas.

> Silas: You ok?

I ignore it and get back in bed. Two hours later, Silas texts again.

> Silas: Are you ignoring me?
> Silas: No problem. Please shoot Selena Benson from the County Council Administrator's office an email. Attach your resume and let her know I recommended you to her regarding a spot on the committee she is putting together. It's a paid position.

> Me: Sorry, I have been in bed all day napping. Thanks a lot. I will send the email first thing tomorrow.
>
> Silas: Cool.

I do as Silas says and send Ms. Benson an email with my resume and a letter of interest. I spend an hour trying to research her, but I couldn't find any pictures of her at events, nor could I find anything other than her name, email address, and position on the County Government's website.

♪ ♪ ♪

For the next few days, I spend half my time sleeping and half of my time online narrowing down the PhD programs I will apply to next. Then, Silas reaches out again.

> Silas: Hey, are you busy tonight at 7pm?

I hate when people ask me if I am busy. My answer depends on what they want.

On one hand, I'm like, *Fuck Silas*. On the other hand, I'm like, *Please, sir, can you get me a job?* While I am trying to construct a polite way to reply, he texts again.

> Silas: My office was invited to hang out in a suite at the baseball game tonight. I can give you one of the tickets. Selena Benson will be there and I can introduce you in person.

Me: Ok, cool! Thanks! I assume it's easy enough to take the bus there?
Silas: Why the bus? There is a parking garage.
Me: Bus money prolly cheaper than gas money.
Silas: If you have enough gas to get to my office, you can ride with me. I'll reimburse you.
Me: That's a lot to ask.
Silas: To go to a baseball game for free and possibly get a job?
Me: No, for you to reimburse me for gas.
Silas: No, it's really not. And you didn't ask. Sounds like you need to swallow your pride and come see about this job.
Me: Shame is a harsh tactic. Thanks.
Silas: You're the one who is always ashamed. This is business. Text me when you get here.

As soon as he sends the address, I take my time getting ready, even curling my hair and using a razor to shape my eyebrows. All these little extra touches because there is a woman I need to impress instead of a hetero man. I am intentional with my business casual, wanting to project non-threatening and serious. So, even as hot as it is, I will wear my one appropriate short-sleeved blouse instead of a sleeveless top.

When I text Silas upon my arrival at the County Administration building, he is already walking into the parking garage. Most of the cars are gone for the day, so we see each other immediately. As he walks up to meet me at my car, he pulls folded bills from his pocket. "Gas money. Put it in your purse now so I don't forget."

This is embarrassing. I want to avoid eye contact. However, it would be worse if I don't look at him.

"I really appreciate it," I say, looking at him sincerely. Without counting it, I put it in the zipper-part of my purse.

He waves me off as if it's nothing and walks me the rest of the way to his car. On the way to the stadium, he talks about the procedure to get the field ready for a baseball game and how cool it is that the suite is behind home plate or some shit. I don't give a shit about any of this. Why is he always chatty about the intricate details of everything?

Once we arrive to the suite in the stadium, the racial makeup presents the most palpable vibe—to me, anyway. Other than the suite attendant and some dopey looking dude who badly needs a shape-up, Silas and I are the only Black people here. The room and its outdoor seating area are lively, and the thirty or so people seem to be having a blast. There is a bar, a buffet, and a VIP air to the place. Silas seems right at home. I thought I was pretty good at code switching, but he is so good that he doesn't even detectably switch. Where the other Black guy is so very Carlton Banks, Silas is basically the same dude he always is around work folks, confident and comfortable. In fact, the other Black dude and Silas do not interact at all.

We both serve ourselves from the buffet and Silas goes back to get us beers after we sit. He can barely get through his food because people are constantly coming up to him with that "Silas, my man!" shit. He introduces me to them all as a graduate student applying to internships with the County.

"You want to sit outside?" he asks when I have finished eating two hamburger sliders, three chicken tenders, and a big ass soft pretzel.

"Not really," I say apologetically.

"Okay, well, I'll be back." He walks outside and stands around talking to people.

As he is finishing up a conversation and about to come back inside, a woman slinks up to him. She has the look of a woman who doesn't care one bit that he is married. Wearing a white sleeveless blouse, mint green jeans, and neutral-colored heels, she has the facial features and skin tone that makes men ask, *Where are you from? What's your background?* Like, for many people, that would be a microaggression, but I bet she has found a way to use the ambiguity to her advantage. She is about my height, so she has to look up to him, but most people here are looking up to him as they talk. This flat-behind trollop is so shameless that she grabs his hand and leads him to a row of seats where they both sit down. She is tossing her black, shoulder-length hair, laughing, chatting away, and doing that annoying thing where every three seconds she tucks her hair behind her ears even though it's already tucked. Thanks, I hate her.

She hogs him for twenty-seven full minutes before someone else sits in the other seat beside her. That guy is clearly interested in her Miss International lookin' ass, whereas Silas maintains a look of professional graciousness. I am relieved when she turns to bask in the new dude's attention and Silas comes back to me—I mean back inside.

"You want another beer?" he asks, walking past me toward the bar.

"Yes, please." I think my tone is cold. I don't feel jealous, just annoyed. And no one has talked to me yet about a job.

Miss International walks into the suite and Silas calls to her, "Miss Benson!"

Fuck. *This* is the Ms. Benson I sent my resume to?

If I had been thinking, I would have taken time to refresh my lipstick and eat a breath mint while I was watching her flirt with Silas. Shit. It's okay. Game face. I'm okay.

"I want you to meet the graduate student I was telling you about," Silas introduces as she walks up to where I am sitting. "This is Roshawn Bell."

"Hi, nice to meet you," we both say as we shake hands.

She switches to business mode—which is to say that there are only stars in her eyes when she looks at Silas. She is looking at me in a situation-appropriate manner: as my potential employer. Polite from a position of power.

"Y'all need at least one young person on that Diversity and Inclusion Committee," coaxes Silas.

Fuck, it's diversity work? No wonder they got spots open. That shit is the fucking worst. I need a job I need a job I need a job.

"You're right, you're right," she concedes, with

her hands up in mock defense. "What are you studying again?" she asks me.

"Social policy," I answer confidently.

"See that?" Silas charms. "Perfect fit. AND she's gettin' Town Council experience over in [REDACTED]."

Whole time, I'm trying to look like I am merely interested in instead of desperate for the job. Also trying not to look like I just called her names in my head or that I'm guessing her age, which I put at about 36, but she seems so much more mature than me.

"Alright, Silas," she chuckles, shaking her head. "Send me your resume," she says, smiling at me.

"I sent it on July 6th," I say, forcing a smile.

"Oh." She cocks her head to the side. "Okay. Well, I'll check for it."

"Thanks." I want out of here.

But she is already onto the next opportunity to hog Silas to herself. "Oh, Silas! We have to talk to Josh, speaking of committees." She grabs his free arm, he grabs his beer, and she practically drags him away.

I gulp down my beer kinda fast. As soon as I'm done, the attendant is standing beside me handing me another one. Is it that obvious, Brother Man? He disappears before I can thank him. Feeling lonely, I decide to go outside to pretend to watch the game. When I reach the door, Brother Man hands me a cone of popcorn and disappears again.

I find a seat outside, put my sunglasses on, and a guy comes and sits next to me. "You're the grad student, right?" he inquires. He's had a few, and I would love to be where he is.

"That's me!" I say cheerfully. Shit, maybe he

knows of a job that's not in diversity work.

"You like baseball?" He's very friendly.

"Honestly, I don't get it," I admit.

"Oh, let me explain it to you!" And he does. For the next hour. When he talks, it sounds like he is bouncing. It's weird. At least he gets me my third drink, which is an actual drank and not a beer, and I don't have to pretend to not be thinking about any possible chemistry between Silas and Miss International.

Then, Silas texts asking if I want to stay or if I am ready to leave. I am so ready to leave. But before I get up, Roy Janowicz gives me his card and tells me to give him a call.

♪ ♪ ♪

When we get in Silas' car, he says, "And don't you dare call Roy."

"You're like a real DAD sometimes, you know that?" I observe.

"Yup." He starts the car and we're on our way.

"Do you have kids?" I ask. The beer mostly gave me a headache, but it's also encouraging my probing.

"Yup. My oldest son is 21. Then I have a 13-year-old son and an 11-year-old son."

"Daaammmnnn." Oops. I sang that out loud.

"What?" He seems mildly offended.

"Nothing." I clean it up. "You look too young to have a 21-year-old."

He shrugs. "As long as I can keep *him* from havin' one too early." We talk a bit more and then he says, "I don't think you should drive. I'ma take you home."

The possibility of Junior or any of our friends seeing us together makes me visibly uncomfortable.

"This was business," he says, reading my mind. "And anyway, speaking of business, they can mind theirs."

Well alright.

Silas gets me home, says goodbye, watches me walk in, and pulls off. Business, just like he said.

9

My mother wakes me up around 7:00am by just barging in my room and repeating my name until I wake up. I know how early it is because she is out the door by 7:15am on workdays. I turn over and perceive a blur of her standing there with one hand on her hip and the other on the doorknob she turned without knocking.

"You seem to be in the habit of drinking too much and having men bring you home," she accuses.

"What?" First of all …

"Where is your car?" she demands.

"At my friend's job. I'll get it later." Fuck is her problem?

"You need to stop drinking." She folds her arms and stares at me.

"Ma, you are trippin'. I'm fine. My friends look out for me."

"And what do you think they think of you? Always having to drive you home?"

Yeah. I gotta get a job and get the fuck back up out of here.

"Have a nice day at work," I throw over my shoulder as I turn back over.

"STOP DRINKING." She slams my door as she leaves my room.

♪ ♪ ♪

By 10am, I have had breakfast and drafted an email to Miss International—I mean, Ms. Benson. She can have Silas. I just need a job and I ain't too proud to beg. Diversity work it is.

> Dear Ms. Benson,
> It was a pleasure to meet you at the baseball game yesterday evening. I am writing to express, again, my strong interest in a position with your office. I am available for a formal interview ~~if necessary, and able to start work immedia~~ ~~am confident that I can accommodate a~~ at your convenience. Please find my resume attached. I look forward to learning more about your work.
> Best,
> Roshawn Bell

It's Friday, and I do not want to be around when my mother gets home from work. Imagine her telling me to stop drinking, but she got Junior Stave droppin' off six-packs. Like, are you kidding me? Speaking of Junior, I haven't heard from him in a minute.

> Me: What's up tonight?
> Junior: Bond got a show at some spot it's a local showcase

His lack of punctuation makes this show come

across as a bad idea. But staying here just to give my mother the cold shoulder all evening is an even worse idea. Do I ask if I can roll with him? Wait for him to invite me?

> Junior: I can send you the info I'm riding with Kai
> Me: Ok.

Wondering whether I'm desperate enough to ask Kai if I can roll, I realize that Silas hasn't hit me about getting my car from his job.

> Me to Silas: Good morning. Are you coming to take me to my car?
> Silas: Good morning. ????
> Me: ????
> Silas: I'm at work.

This asshole.

> Silas: You don't have anyone to take you to your car? Call Junior.

Ass. Hole.

> Me to Junior: Can you take me to

Oh shit. If I ask Junior to take me to the County Administration building, he will know I went out with Silas. Fuck. *Delete.*

I get a text from an unknown number.

> Unknown number: Ro this is Sharmel. Junior said you want to go to the show

Ah, another option. Roll with the ladies again. I do need to get out of here tonight.

> Me: Hey Sharmel!

Sharmel sends an image of the flyer for the show. I count 11 different rappers' names on this thing, and none sound familiar. Hold up… *Cover: $10*. What the hell? I don't want to pay $10 to see these fools I don't even know! And I still have to get my car. If I wasn't so worried about Junior knowing where my car was, I could get him to pay my $10 cover. Shit. Oh, well.

> Me: I want to go, but I don't have my car.
> Sharmel: We got room if you want to ride with us

She's so sweet. If I go with them tonight, I could still see if Silas can take me to my car tomorrow.

Wait! Silas gave me gas money! I can give them a few dollars to take me to my car before or after the show.

I run to the living room to get my purse and yank open the zipper on the outer pocket. When I pull out the folded bills, I count five twenties and three hundreds.

Silas gave me FOUR HUNDRED DOLLARS.

> Me: Yes, please! And I can give whoever

> gas money to take me to my car! It's
> not far!
> Sharmel: OK let me let Dink know

Dink as in Dinko? I damn near jump out of my skin.

"Shit shit shit shit shit shit shit shit shit shit shit shit shit," I say out loud, as I stomp back to my room—a "shit" for each time my foot pounds the carpeted floor. Inside my room, I fall onto the bed. Oh my gawd. Breathe.

Oh, wait. Does Dinko know Silas works at the County Administration Building?

♪ ♪ ♪

Stretch pants. Stretch pants, right? It's just some rappers anyhow, and I can give Dinko a good view of the goods. What about easy access, though? What if I have another opportunity for him to *touch* me? Suppose it's in his car? But I can't really justify putting on a skirt for local rappers. Junior will be there too. Shit. I can't look like I am trying too hard, then—especially since I will be walking in with Dinko. Stretch pants with a short-enough but loose-enough top. Sandals? Ugh, for the rappers? Nah, I have some low-top Nikes around here somewhere. Do I need curls in my hair? Nah, the sweaty young rap crowd would have it humid in there. I have a few hours. I can wash it and wrap it.

By the time my mother pulls up blasting Teena Marie, I am sitting under the dryer. I didn't intend to speak to her, and I am glad she didn't come back to my room to speak to me. She went upstairs to her room and didn't come back down before I left. According to Sharmel, they'll be picking me up at 8:00pm.

♪ ♪ ♪

At 7:30, I remember to eat, so I microwave three leftover chicken wings. Microwaved chicken is disgusting, so I eat two Hostess CupCakes to get that taste out of my mouth.

At 8:05, I remember to chew some gum in case I had chocolate on my teeth.

At 8:37, I am kneeling on the living room sofa, peering out of the curtain at the window, finishing half a bag of barbecue potato chips. A white van with *Brown & Brown Remodeling* and a phone number on its side pulls up. Just as I am wondering if my mother is having company, my text alert chimes.

Sharmel: We here

Ew. Okay. I take my time putting my phone into my wristlet in case this is NOT them in the work van. I don't look at the driver until I have locked the front door and am walking down the porch steps toward the truck.

Dinko is driving. He looks at me and smiles that easy smile, setting off the butterflies in the spot between my chest and stomach.

So, of course I trip on the very last step and almost fall face forward to the ground.

"You a'ight?" Dinko asks with a furrowed brow.

"Yes," I answer, shaking my head.

"Get in on the other side," he says.

Bond is standing by the open side door. I climb into the back, and Sharmel is sitting on what looks to be a stack of floor tiles. As Bond closes the door, she says, "You can sit on the crate," pointing to an upside-down red crate beside the door that was just closed.

No, we will not be fucking Dinko in the back of the Brown & Brown Remodeling van.

Are we sure?

On our way to the venue in the city, Bond is playing his own tracks from his phone. It sounds very much like every other 20-something rapper, mostly nonsense and sounding high and choppy and slurry at the same time. I must be an old lady, because this fucking sucks.

He, however, is rapping along like this is the shit. Poor Sharmel is the perfect picture of the struggling artist's girlfriend. The look on her face is supposed to be frozen in constant assurance that she likes his music, she is supportive of his dreams, and that she is confident that he can—no, he *should*—be rich and famous.

By the time she blurts out the lyrics, *Finger guns up in the air / and we bussin off / Raise your L up in the air / and we [cough, cough]*, I can't tell whether it's because she's heard it two million times and can't help rapping along to the hook or because she really thinks he's spittin hot fire.

At 80 degrees outside and the windows down instead of air conditioning, it is surprisingly cool in the back of the van. We park in the lot across the street from the venue, and instead of getting out, Dinko and Bond make their way into the back with us. They sit on the floor of the van and both light up long spliffs. They have positioned themselves in a way where we make four points of a diamond, so when they complete their two pulls, they each pass to their right so we can puff. I am not enthused that I am to Bond's right, but I will forget all about this after the first rotation.

Bond checks his phone. "Kai and June already in there."

Shit, sitting here next to the man of my most lustful dreams and having $200 of Silas' $400 on me, I forgot that Junior even existed. Sharmel passes to Bond. When I pass to Dinko, I keep my fingers right in the middle between the lit end and the pulling end so he will have to touch my fingers to take it from me.

The touch of his thick, warm fingers on mine is like the strum of a bass, plucking what I can only assume is my cervix. Good God almighty, maybe he is my ONE. I can't imagine the last time I was so *affected* by a man.

"I'm proud o' ol' June, man," Bond breathes after a pull. "Keepin' it movin'."

Dinko and Sharmel nod, and I wonder what he means by that.

"I'm just glad they talkin' again," says Sharmel.

"No bullshit," adds Dinko, passing to her.

Bond passes to me. "Friends is friends, business is business," he quips.

Another hit takes away my ability to refrain from asking details. "What are y'all talkin' about?"

"June and Silas," Sharmel answers before an exhale.

I damn near drop the blunt. Uh oh. I recover by

taking a big toke and letting myself have a couple of coughs before handing it to Dinko. The coughing spins my head even more. Fuck it, now I gotta know. "What happened?" I inquire.

"You didn't know?" Bond looks genuinely confused. "Silas laid him off?"

Laid him off. What does that mean?

"His father sold the company," Sharmel explains. "He had to."

"That was fucked up though," Dinko mutters on an exhale.

This explains a lot.

"We can get free massages now," giggles Sharmel.

Dinko snaps, "WE?!" as Bond chokes out, "WE WHO?"

"Okay, well *I* can, then!" Sharmel laughs.

"Oh hell no you can't!" Bond doesn't like that one bit. "Finger-Me Foster know better than THAT!"

Sharmel and I catch a case of the giggles. How Dinko is keeping a straight face is beyond me.

"A'ight, let's hit the stage!" Dinko ordered.

Bond switches gears immediately, extinguishing his blunt in an old ceramic ashtray that I didn't even notice was on the floor in the middle of us.

"Wait! Lemme get another pull!" The words are out of my mouth before I can stop them. Dinko, my hero, hands his to me. I do a double pull like it's my last hope and they all stare at me. Is this amusement or pity, I wonder as I hold my breath? Shit, it's both, I realize as I let the smoke out.

Walking across the parking lot wanting to feel cute, I realize that with all the eating I had to get in before I left, I never put on lipstick. I didn't even put a tube in my wristlet. I am so busy being absolutely bothered by Dinko that I am not slowing down enough to be cool about it. An affirmation I read once comes to mind: *One's ships come in over a calm sea.*

Calm. Down.

The person working the door asked if we wanted to show our IDs to get wristbands to drink. Now you know if a place has to give out wristbands for drinking, there are people here who are not yet old enough to drink. My old-lady factor increases.

The place is one of those standing-only venues, and a good enough size to put on a show starring eleven local rappers. The eleven of them make up a fourth of the audience. One is already on the stage, sounding to me exactly like Bond in his songs. Besides me and Sharmel, I count maybe twelve other women. Ten of them look young as hell, and two are probably moms of the rappers. The men vary in age, but only three or four appear to be over 35.

Oh, here come Junior and Kai. Make that six who appear to be over 35.

As they walk up and greet us, Junior gives me a regular nod and a "Wha'sup" like I'm just any-ol'-body. I should be offended, but I guess I am glad he doesn't look like he suspects or even cares that I rolled in with Dinko—well, Dinko, Sharmel, and Bond. In fact, as we all politely head-nod our way through the next couple of acts, Junior Stave doesn't give me anything. No glances, no conversation, no drink. I am not used to not being taken care of by Junior.

The DJ is playing mellow hip hop classics on a break, and I can finally enjoy this high instead of leaning on it to get through these acts. I bask in the nostalgia of lyrics I can feel (and understand) and the connection to only a few other people in the place who can remember when hip hop was this good.

I hear the opening to Mos Def's "Ms. Fat Booty," and I take my fat booty over to Junior. I think I want a drink, and I think he should get me one. I take his hand and groove, keeping about a foot's distance between us. He starts moving to the beat but is playing it pretty cool. What's up with that?

I take his other hand and keep most of my motion in my hips. By the second verse, I give up on seduction and start clowning instead, rapping along and acting out the lyrics. ♪ *Traced her arms across my shoulder blades.* He loosens up. ♪ *Got the folded fingers on her waist.* When I have him laughing, I turn around to make him really feel the phat. ♪ *Showin me her tan line and her tattoo.* Like many men before him, he falls in line pressed up against my cheeks. The song fades out right after, *She tellin me commitment is somethin she can't manage.*

I look up at the stage and Bond is at the mic. It's about time. I look around for Dinko but can't find him anywhere. Shit, all my playin' in Junior's face may have made him get as far away from me as he could. Did I just fuck this up?

When Bond's first track starts, Dinko bounds from out of nowhere, his large presence commanding the stage as he shouts, "Let's get it on! Word is Bond! Let's get it on! Word is Bond!" He is Bond's hype man and is doing a damn good job of making this set hype.

Bond starts with a song about "money hungry hoes" that makes people laugh with a few funny lines. It's not so bad. Maybe you gotta be high to like it? He segues into the next song, and he truly has the audience in a way that none of the ones who came before him did. More people have arrived to the spot, and the atmosphere has electrified.

I recognize his next song from the ride over here—the one Sharmel was rapping along to. I see her up near the front being his number one fan. To my surprise, people in the crowd seem to know this song, and I can hear a some rapping along. When he gets to the hook, mostly all of them yell along, *"Finger guns up in the air, and we bussin off! Raise your L up in the air, and we [cough, cough]!"* They even doin' the finger guns in the air and fake-coughing on the cough part. Wow. It looks like our boy Bond has a bit of a following. This is some cool shit.

After one more song, we join the crowd in cheers as he thanks everyone for showing him so much love. It takes about 15 minutes for him and Dinko to get back to us in the audience. After dapping them up, Kai and Junior say their goodbyes to us. I guess they just wanted to support Bond and then get the hell out of there.

For a while, people are coming up to Bond, giving him dap and promising to connect. When I see a girl come up and tell Dinko, "Y'all were the best out of everybody!" I have to step in and stake a claim.

While the girl is still standing there with a look of expectation on her face, I beckon him with my forefinger and say, "Come here." He steps forward and leans down to put his ear by my mouth. "Can I reward you for that good show?" I tease.

He freezes for a second then stands straight up again, looking off into the distance as if he is thinking. I quickly grab his hand and start dancing, because the DJ is giving up some Dirty South nasties and more women have shown up to the place. With all the titties and asses bouncing around at this point, I need to lock Dinko down.

I slip my wristlet further up my arm so I can grab his other hand and grind right up on him as "Some Cut" by Trillville booms. ♪ *What it is ho, what's up?* I bring both of his hands around and give him two hands full of ass and then reposition my arms so I can grip the wristlet and keep my hands on his broad shoulders. ♪ *Well gimme your number and I'll call.* Yes, I do need to get this man's number.

"Hey, you need to gimme your number!" I yell up to him over the music.

"Come outside," he responds as he stops dancing.

He heads straight for the door and I am right on his heels. He pauses for the splittest of seconds to light a cigarette then keeps going toward the parking lot.

Oh. I think we will be having work van sex tonight.

He isn't walking too fast or slow, but his pace is steady. He's not even looking back at me to see where I am. I guess he can hear me panting as I try to keep up with his stride. We are about ten feet away from the van and he uses a key fob to unlock the doors. I swear, I'ma actually jump on his ass when we get inside.

A bellow of "Bitch ass nigga!" is the first sign of a

ruckus that escalates exponentially from that point. We turn around and see that, across the street, a crowd is bursting out of the venue's front doors.

"Oh shit," we both say out loud.

Dinko starts walking fast back in that direction. "Where my cousin at?"

Someone runs from the crowd into the middle of the street shrieking, "What's up now, nigga?!" and putting his hands up and bucking at the crowd. And then Bond runs up out of nowhere and clocks dude right in the grill.

"Bond!" Dinko runs over and grabs Bond as a couple of other dudes run up on him, swinging.

Dinko is only worried about getting Bond away, but then one of them hits him. Dinko knocks the dude out cold.

"Oh, that's a'ight!" yells one dude. "Stay right there, I got sumpm for you!" He starts walking fast toward the parking lot.

Dinko and Bond chase dude to the parking lot, knock him down, and get in a few more hits to keep him down.

Sharmel runs past them and is headed my way. I open the back door of the van and we climb in.

Two seconds later, Dinko runs up and shuts the door, he and Bond jump into the front, Dinko starts it up, and we roll out fast.

When Dinko feels like he has put in enough distance, he slows down. "Last thing we need is to get pulled over for speeding," he grumbles.

I can feel all four of our hearts racing, and I can hear all of us trying to get our breathing back to a normal pace.

"FUCK, man!" roars Bond, pounding the dashboard with his fist.

"Careful, man!" Dinko scolds. "Don't fuck up my shit!"

Bond collapses into his seat.

"What the fuck happened?" Dinko asks.

"Remember dem niggas was mad we took their spot?"

"Them *wack* ass niggas?"

"Yeah, man, dey was talkin' shit. I told 'em I ain't have nothin' to do with it. Sammy even told 'em … people know my songs, don't nobody know dem. Dey can't follow me on no stage, man."

Dinko shakes his head. "What the fuck, man. We don't need this shit, man."

"I know!"

I glance at Sharmel. She has her head in her hands, massaging her forehead. We are both sitting on the floor of the van with our knees up.

"Ay shorty, I'ma drop you off at your house," Dinko says with enough direction to let me know he is talking to me. "I gotta get my cousin home."

10

My grandfather was somewhat of an underground local legend. People respected and feared him, and after his death, they romanticized his life and his influence. Moving one state over allowed my mother to escape only the most immediate vestiges of his impact. However, she still had to move to a place that held some connection, because my father, having worked for my grandfather, set it up for her.

When I started elementary school, I didn't have any friends. I knew immediately that people had been warned about my family or been told stories and rumors that we got people killed or something. It was never really confirmed, but I think people told their kids to stay away from me. Kaia became my friend because her mother never really looked out for them. Kai was her parent, and her being my friend gave her something to do other than be up under him.

I was a very well-behaved kid, though, and once I discovered that no one expected anything other than crime from me, I did everything I could to be the opposite of my family reputation. I was always among the top achievers in my classes, highly awarded, and eventually, highly respected. When I wasn't pushing myself to prove that I was worthy of approval, my mother was shrouding me in respectability.

Once Kaia and I started showing interest in boys, she lectured us constantly about not having sex. Of course, that only increased my interest in it. Unfortunately, Ma would only buy me clothes that bordered on homely—nothing too tight, short, sheer, or trendy. She didn't want me to draw attention to myself in any way except academically, which I was already handling. While other teens were going to parties, going to the mall by themselves, and hanging out with friends, Kaia and I were going to the movies, going to the mall, and hanging out with my mother. Kaia loved it, as she had the mother she was missing. For me, being plainly dressed and accompanied everywhere by my mother, in addition to being labeled a teacher's pet in school, made me undesirable to boys. Even when we were able to ditch my mother and go with Kai up to the basketball court, those guys knew what was up.

Kai was probably just flattering me when he used to tell the other boys, "Leave them alone." Kaia was the one they always talked to. She was naturally pretty, with long, thick hair and perfect long eyelashes. Her hair, skin, and eyes were the same shade of honey brown and people were always staring at her. Shit, my mother was probably just flattering me too; her hawkish watching of us probably did Kaia more good than it did me.

My mother encouraged both of us to go to an HBCU because she wasn't allowed to. Kaia and I got into the same one, in-state, and my mother was so proud. She trusted that she had set us on the right path and that we would have each other's backs once we got there.

Like many of our counterparts, hormones took over upon being set loose among an entirely new community of young people bursting into their new phase of life as college students. I was secretly thrilled that our request to be roommates was not honored, because our paths diverged almost immediately when we settled into our new lives on campus.

That first week of school in September 1995, two sophomores from New York charmed us with their exotic accents and attitudes. Of course, she got the more handsome one and I got the other one, his roommate. Her goody-two-shoes ways didn't hold that guy's attention, but my eagerness to break free surely kept Akil's attention. I didn't quite believe his Five Percenter philosophies, but he introduced me to weed, hours-long makeout sessions, and pseudo-intelligent conversations about Afrocentric books and authors. He insisted that I call him Born (full name Born God Supreme or Born Supreme Islam, I forget), and I insisted that he be my first sexual partner. Aside from all of his posturing and preaching, he was incredibly sensual and I loved the way he smelled. The only time I ever saw him scared was when I told him that he would be my first. It was October before he would even consider handling what he called "too much responsibility."

Meanwhile, my Sociology 101 class was with a 28-year-old adjunct professor whose life outside of teaching was local activism and freelance journalism. When I look back on it, he is the one who set me on the course for wanting to study social policy. If there was one thing I had spent years perfecting by that point, it was being a teacher's pet. Courtney's boyishly handsome, tall, skinny, afro-haired self didn't stand a chance with me, especially since it was his first semester teaching, and he only had the one class. There were plenty of interesting talks and artsy happenings on campus, and I stayed giving him flyers and telling him that he should show up to support the students. I appealed to his save-the-youth optimism, and he did start spending a lot more time on campus.

My making a big deal about turning 18 on November 10th proved to be the kryptonite that weakened both Courtney and Akil. I had to work a bit harder on Courtney after he attended the Million Man March and got righteous for a few weeks. As I spent a few weeks deciding which one would be the lucky guy, I made a pros and cons list in my head that I shared with Kaia.

"I already came so close with Born so many times, it may as well be him," I told Kaia.

"He seems sketchy to me," Kaia said. "I stopped dealing with Rob a long time ago. Them dudes sell weed."

"Shoot, that's in Born's 'pros' column!" I laughed.

"That weed must be clouding your vision. He is not all that."

No shit, I was thinking. *You took the fine one.*

"Courtney is older, I bet he has more experience," I sighed.

Kaia sneered. "Courtney?"

"*All* of his students call him Courtney."

She scrunched up her face. "Why you want some

old man taking your virginity?"

"Twenty-eight is not an old man," I declared, when it hit us both at the same time: *Like mother, like daughter.* We both skipped right on past that part.

"He's your professor though," she continued. "There must be a rule against it or something."

"If it's love, there ain't no rules." I couldn't even say it with confidence.

"You love him?" Kaia asked in a way that let me know she already knew I was joking.

"I'm just READY."

"Well, wait 'til you get some better prospects, then." Spoken like a pretty girl who was never, ever without a boy or man panting in her face. If I were her, I would be waiting too.

♪ ♪ ♪

My birthday fell on a Friday. Akil/Born won the contest he didn't even know he was in by promising me a candlelight dinner at his off-campus apartment. He said his roommate, Rob, would be out for the night so we could make this a truly special occasion. Courtney lost out by not being available until that Sunday night.

Akil picked me up from campus, drove the short distance to his apartment, and left me there while he drove Rob somewhere. I was expecting him back within an hour, but three hours later, I had heard nothing from him. I know I paged him twenty times with my *1110* code.

Another hour passed before I heard a knock on the door. I looked out of the peephole and saw a police officer. My heart dropped. I just knew the officer was coming to say that Akil had been in an accident and was dead. I opened the door, and several more officers pushed past me into the apartment.

The leader of the police gang told me to have a seat and asked me questions about Akil while the others searched the apartment. He wore a cream-colored Eddie Bauer waffle-knit sweater, baggy jeans, butter Timbs, and his badge on a chain. Imagine any picture of Wu-Tang Clan from the 90s, and he would fit right in. By the end of his interrogation, I had learned more about Akil/Born. He was 23 years old, not 20 like he told me, not even a college student, and the weed selling was connected to more than just a small-time quick cash grab.

In my desperate attempt to walk away from the whole thing without a trip to jail or a call to my mother, I cried about it being my 18th birthday and threw in, "I was supposed to have sex for the first time tonight."

The plainclothes Detective Wallace was kind to me. He was empathetic to my situation and naivete, insinuating that they had been watching Akil and Rob long enough to know I was just some college girl he saw sometimes. Still, he took down all my information saying, "So you remember to stay out of trouble."

The next night, Bradford Wallace came to pick me up from my dorm. I didn't find him handsome when I thought I was going to jail, but he got more handsome when I realized he was having mercy on me. He got even more handsome when I called him earlier that day and he acted like that was the most natural thing in the world. He was absolutely finger-licking fine as he sat across a candle-lit dining table in a long-sleeved black Ralph Lauren Polo shirt with khakis and black Timbs. Instead of the badge around his neck, he wore a gold Cuban link chain. At the elegant restaurant he took me to, I was not carded when he ordered a bottle of wine for us. He was very charming, different from both Akil and Courtney, who didn't have to work too hard with me because I was so hungry for their attention. Bradford's conversation was exceptionally easy, and he made me feel more mature than Akil or Courtney ever did.

The restaurant was next door to a plush hotel, the likes of which I haven't seen since. When we walked through its grand doors, I expected to have to linger back while he booked us a room, but he took my hand and led me straight to the elevator. In the elevator, we were alone. He pushed me up against the mirrored wall and looked into my eyes. When I reached up to pull his face to mine, he pulled back, gently grabbed my hands, and held them at my sides while he continued staring into my eyes. If we had ascended any further than the 6th floor where we got off, they would have needed to mop up after me.

He had already decorated the room with three dozen red roses in vases and red rose petals on the king-size bed. There were two white velour robes laid across the bed's white comforter. "Get comfortable," he said, walking over to the cd player he had set on the dresser and hitting play on Jon B's *Bonafide*.

I sat on the bed, not wanting to take anything off while the lights in the room were on, but he took off his shirt. I had had enough wine to not think about forcing my gaze away from his muscles. Instead, I let my eyes drink him in so that he would know I appreciated every single one of them.

"You got anything to drink?" I asked.

"You want water or juice?" he replied, retrieving one juice and one water from the mini fridge. He saw the disappointment on my face and added, "I don't wanna do nothin' you need to be drunk for."

"Oh, naw, I was just asking," I conceded, accepting the water from him. I opened it and took a sip, just to have something to do with my hands.

He took the water bottle from me and walked around the bed to set it and the juice bottle on the nightstand. "You okay?"

"Yeah," I answered with confidence. "Can we turn the lights off or something?"

He chuckled and turned the lights off, then walked to the big window and opened the curtain so the city lights could add to the ambiance of the darkened room. When he got back to the bed, he knelt down and took my block-heeled boots and socks off, then stood up and pulled me to standing. He pulled my turtleneck over my head and paused to smooth my hair back down.

I reached up and pulled his face toward mine, but he drew back again. He pulled down my stretch pants and got on one knee to help me out of them. Even though I was wearing a new orange bra and underwear set, my hands instinctively went to cover myself, but he held them and started kissing my thighs. ♪ *It's because of you I was able to give my heart again. You give me someone to love.* He worked his way straight to my underwear and started kissing my lips through the satin. My knees went numb as he brought my hands around to the sides of his head and didn't let go until I gripped his head firmly enough. He kept kissing and gently nibbling while holding the backs of my thighs.

"Pleeaase…" I moaned.

"Please what?" he whispered, looking up at me.

I looked back at the bed then back down at him. "Please, come on."

"Please what?" he whispered again.

"Put me on the bed please."

He got up and grasped my shoulders to give me a light push back on the bed. I eased myself further back and got under the covers while he sat down and calmly took off his pants, shoes, and socks. When he got under the covers with me, I reached for him immediately, but he shoved my shoulder back to the bed with minor effort and held me there. Once he felt me relax and was satisfied that I would play his game, he traced down my body with his fingertips. I eagerly opened my legs, but when he got to my clit he stopped.

I was breathing hard. "Please," I begged.

"Please what?" he whispered.

"Please touch me."

In a series of swift motions, he pulled the covers back, knelt between my legs, pulled off my panties, and went at my clit with his tongue instead. I haven't had any other man since him give me head that good. He knew exactly how to suck, with exactly the right pressure, with exactly the right rhythm, and I came within a minute. As I gasped for breath, he moved up to kiss me, circling my tongue with his, sucking and biting my bottom lip, and finally, reaching behind me to take off my bra. Sitting up slightly so he could pull my bra off, I lunged for the band of his boxer briefs, and he pushed me back down and kept kissing me.

Hey Pretty Girl, can I be your man tonight?

"Please," I murmured into his mouth.

"Please what?"

"Put it in," I commanded.

He stopped kissing me just long enough to take off his boxer shorts, then positioned himself between my legs and started kissing me again. I reached down and wrapped my hand around his big, hard dick and enjoyed a final few moments of virginity, stroking him tenderly enough to switch the game up on him. Jon B was wondering, *How does a man like me seduce a girl like you?*

There was no hesitation, no 'Please' or 'Please what?' He glided inside, groaning, "Oh my god," moving as slowly as possible into my tightness. It didn't hurt as badly as I had expected it to, but it probably would have been more uncomfortable if I hadn't been so excited by the everything of it all. He remained gentle with me, kissing me softly and asking if I was okay as he finessed in long strokes.

As his climax was building, he gripped my chin firmly and looked into my eyes. "You belong to me?"

"Yes," I moaned through clenched teeth. "Yes!"

He came yelling, "Fuuuuck!"

The next morning, he took me to breakfast at a diner. I was over the moon in love, but I knew it wasn't time to tell him that. I did want to know one thing, though. "How old are you?" I inquired.

"How old do you want me to be?" he said without emotion, not even taking his eyes off the menu.

11
Marshawn

There's book smarts and there's street smarts. But underlying the thing they call street smarts is plain ass common sense. But it ain't that common, and Roshawn's dumb ass sure don't have it. I know I should not call my only child a dumbass, because it's all my fault. I spent so much time trying to keep her safe, but I always kick myself for not letting her figure some things out earlier on in life. Then again, with the chance to figure things out earlier, she would have come home pregnant after just starting high school instead of when she first started college.

  Kaia called me every other day when they went away to school. They were only two hours from here, which was close enough for my comfort but far enough away where I could finally have a life mostly to myself again. Kaia was my baby. All she needed was some direction and some love, and she turned out just fine. Her parents were a hot ass mess, and her mother only had Kai and then her to try to keep her father around. It didn't work. That woman didn't want them kids. So, how did the dumbass woman have two smart kids, but the smart woman had a dumbass kid? The Lord works in mysterious ways.

I say this proud that I wasn't brought up in a church with the Bible shoved down my throat, and I didn't raise Roshawn that way, either. You want to see the snakes and predators of the world, look in the religious places. That's what my father always said. But, still, there's the thing called common sense, and it also dictates that you should bring your child up on a straight and narrow path and they will stay on it. I had them girls so straight that they both got full-ride scholarships to college. So what happened to Ro?

Book smart people debate 'nature versus nurture' when individuals go off their given paths. When a person does some shit, is it because of something hereditary that determined they were destined to do that shit? Or did they do the shit because of something that happened while they were growing up? Back when I went to college, we learned that it's not either-or, nature or nurture, but it's *both* and *then some*. My questions since having to raise Roshawn's dumb ass are: How long can you outrun genetics? And, will the past always catch up?

Like I said, Kaia called me all the time, so I knew what was going on with Ro even when she didn't know I knew. When I could catch her on her dorm room phone, I would get some details, so I had heard about the Muslim dude, Prince Akeem, or whoever. Besides, she had been talking about books and social issues since spending time with him, so I didn't think anything of it. College is for exploring, and I knew that when she turned 18, I would lose a lot more control in her life.

A few times when Kaia asked me if she could come to my house on the weekend, Ro said she wanted to stay on campus. There was always an event, a party, a dance, a protest, anything to keep her from coming back this way. I saw her on Thanksgiving break and I could tell she had been through some things—penises, probably—and I had the conversation about birth control pills with both of them. I told them about Planned Parenthood and, in Ro's case, our health insurance, and begged them to start taking them as soon as possible.

Then, they come home Christmas break and Ro is sick and Kaia is giving me the puppy-dog eyes because she is scared to tell me that Ro is pregnant.

"Did that Muslim dude get you pregnant?" I asked her directly as she stood in the kitchen guzzling Seagram's ginger ale.

"No," she said, looking guilty and stupid.

"I think you're pregnant. Who is the father, and does he know?"

She's a terrible liar. She stopped drinking and stood there thinking of an answer to give me.

"Do you not KNOW who the father is?" I questioned, my voice rising.

"She knows!" interjected Kaia walking up behind me. "She just doesn't want to get him in trouble."

"Get WHO in trouble?" My head turned from side to side to look at them both.

"Got damn, Kaia," Ro sighed. "He's a guy from school," she said, setting her ginger ale on the counter.

"And why would he be in trouble?" I tried to

bring my voice down because I could see they were scared shitless.

Kaia and Ro spoke to each other silently, only using their eyes. "He's a professor," Kaia blurted.

"Oh, HELL NO!" I yelled. "I DIDN'T SEND Y'ALL TO THAT SCHOOL FOR SOME PERVERT PROFESSORS TO TAKE ADVANTAGE OF Y'ALL! NOW I GOTTA GO UP THERE AND SHOW MY ASS!"

I was only trying to make my way to the living room sofa to catch my breath, but the way Kaia and Ro tackled me, you would think I was on my way up to the school to get the guy right that second. "No! No!" they screamed. "No, it's okay! Please!"

When we all finally settled back down after I threatened to beat their asses, they explained to me that the father of Ro's baby was a young, adjunct professor who was barely older than they were. I felt only slightly better about that because I know Ro. I know for a fact that Roshawn went after him, not the other way around.

I had a few men I dated as Ro was growing up. She didn't know about most of them because I kept it that way. I could have lunch dates during the workday and evening dates when I sent her to her Aunt Zelda sometimes. When she was about 14, I figured she was old enough to handle the fact that I was dating. The first man I let come to the house was a firefighter I met at a club one night. He was fine-fine, like they probably put him in a fireman calendar back then. Ro and Kaia used to giggle and blush when he came around, but I didn't have any worries that he would try to get with a child. He was very into me, and I was 8 years older than him. Anyway, I should have been watching Roshawn's hot-to-trot ass.

He was standing on the porch waiting for me one day while I was upstairs in my room finishing up getting ready. There is one thing that I have always noticed my whole life—one thing I have long since stopped warning people about because they don't believe me or don't remember—and it's that a conversation held just outside of a house can usually be heard inside the house, especially if there is an upstairs to listen from. I heard everything standing by my window upstairs.

On this day, I heard the screen door open and close, then I heard Roshawn say, "Hey."

My firefighter waited at least a second before saying, "Hey," and then, "Ain't you cold?"

Roshawn said, "No," and then, "You got any cigarettes?"

He said, "If I did, I wouldn't give you none."

She said, "Why not?"

He said, "Girl, get in the house before you catch pneumonia." It was one of those surprisingly cold days in March when everybody is desperately waiting for spring to arrive.

She said, "I just came to say hi."

He said, "Goodbye."

I went downstairs fast because all that was just weird as hell. As I get to the bottom of the stairs, this little tramp is coming in the house in a sports bra with no shirt over it, and the Joe Boxer underwear she begged me to buy her the week before was on full display out of the top of her jeans, which were barely over her hips.

"WHAT THE HELL YOU GOT ON?" I roared.

"My Joe Boxers, calm down," she said nonchalantly.

"THAT IS YOUR UNDERWEAR, NOT AN OUTFIT!"

"It is not underwear! You so corny, you don't even know what's in style!"

She was on the ground holding her face, next thing I knew. I guess I knocked her down. "Go in your room and don't come out!"

I waited until she was in her room and then called Zelda to come over and keep an eye on her while I went out. I had considered staying in that night, but if she was flaunting and flirting with my man, she would be too glad if we weren't going out, and I was not going to let her win that one.

I know I have made some mistakes along the way, but I did my best. All I want is for her to do the same.

After I thought about it, I felt sorry for the guy who got Ro pregnant. The only other thing that made me feel better was that she didn't want to keep the baby. I guess her newfound freedom was too good to let go. Her pregnancy was terminated before she went back for the spring semester.

12

Marshawn's inconsiderate ass is going to have to stop barging in my room at the crack of dawn.

"Where is your car?" she demands.

I don't have the strength or the shame anymore. "At the County Building," I say without turning over.

"WHAT county building?"

"The Admin building."

"Get up," she orders. "We're going to get it now."

"Ma, I can…"

"GET UP." She storms out of my room.

I just had to do this to myself. I just had to move back here and be her fucking child again, in my old bedroom. This was not how this was supposed to go.

On the ride to get my car, she is silent. Right before I get out of her car she says, "I know you insist on learning every damn thing the hard way, but don't keep dragging more and more shit into your life."

♪ ♪ ♪

After last night's Town Meeting where I listened to the senior citizens complain without being paid for it,

I grew even more restless. When the hell is Ms. Selena Benson going to get back to me?

I stopped cooking dinner for my mother after last weekend. This week, I ate what I could between 12noon when I got out of bed until around the time she got home, then stayed in my room, out of sight until I knew she was asleep for the night. Then, I would get up and eat again, watch television, and search graduate programs until I fell asleep. I even got a jump on writing a general personal statement for my applications that I can tailor for each school.

Silas seems to be the man with the plan. Let me stop fucking around and get in on it.

> Me: I apologize for not taking the time to thank you for your life-saving generosity.
> Silas: You're welcome. I hope it helps.
> Me: Definitely. I am going to use some for a hotel room tonight. Things are not good here.

Silas doesn't text back. He was staying at a hotel that one night he invited me up to his room. I'm tryna see what's up with that, as in, if he can get me a room there or let me stay in his.

My text alert chimes and it's Sharmel. I am excited about the possibility of having a girl-friend again. Men are a dime a dozen, but a good girl to hang with is hard to find. No one has ever had my back like Kaia did, but Sharmel is a good person.

```
Sharmel: Dinko said you tryna smoke?
Me: Umm... yes!
Sharmel: LOL
Sharmel: He said he got a connect but need
         to buy a half ounce. You got 30$
         on it?
Me: Yeah, I can do that.
Sharmel: Meet us at the house.
Me: Whose house?
Sharmel: Bond and Dinko house
Me: Where is that?
```

♪ ♪ ♪

Do you know that Dinko has been living around the corner from me this whole fucking time? Sharmel gave me the address, and I can walk there. But I'll be damned if I show up sweaty from walking. I will show up fresh and clean and he can make me sweat later.

I get dressed and drive approximately thirty seconds to Dinko's house. It is one of the smallest on his block and looks just a tad more ... hmm, raggedy? ... than the others. I mean, it's a brick house, but it looks kinda gloomy. They need a power wash and some paint on them shutters. I can't pull into the driveway because there is already a car in it with a tarp over it and then another car parked in front of that. I park just outside of the driveway in a spot obscured by some overgrown weedy bushes. Are these bushes on their property? Must be, because on both sides of this house, the other lawns are well-manicured.

As I walk up on the house, the lawn smells musty.

It smells like the sun doesn't shine on it and like, maybe, people piss here? I hear Sharmel's laugh coming from around back, so I head on around. In addition to her, Bond, and *take me now*, Dinko in a beater and basketball shorts, there are two more guys standing around chatting. I say, "Hey," and they all say, "Wha'sup."

Dinko, leaning on the railing to the back steps calls out to me, "Ay, you got that 30?"

I pull it out of my wristlet before I remember to be offended that I didn't get a smile, hug, or thanks before he asked. He gets up and comes to me, takes it, and counts it in with the money he is holding before giving it to one of the strangers in exchange for a paper bag.

"A'ight, man," the stranger says before he and his partner say goodbye and leave.

"Split that for me, cuz," Dinko says. Bond and Sharmel go in the house with the bag, and it's just me, Dinko, and whatever this dank ass smell is in the backyard. However, his attention goes to his phone, not to me.

I get it. He has to play it cool. I mean, look at him. The blue light from the phone is glowing across his face and showing off the contour of his cheekbones, his nose ring is sparkling. He must be swimming in all the pussy thrown his way. I see a few dirty-looking chairs around, but I am hesitant to sit down. Shit, even *he* isn't sitting in one of them.

"You got any OFF?" I ask.

"Any what?" He looked up with a raised eyebrow.

"OFF spray? For the mosquitoes, to keep them off."

He chuckles. "Nah."

"You know, you never did give me your phone num—" Just when I was about to pick up where we left off the last time, Sharmel comes out the back door.

"She pullin' up," Sharmel says.

From where I am around back, I can see headlights pulling up on the street in front of the house. Shortly after, I hear a car door shut. Dinko never looked up from his phone. Bond comes out the back door and says, "We good."

And then, a knife to my gut as Nikki walks into the backyard.

Dammit. So now I gotta play it off and smile in this chick's face like her presence is not totally blocking my plans with her ex. We all say our wha'sups and Bond hands her a baggie with a quarter ounce of weed in it that she puts in the front pocket of her thin, sleeveless hoodie.

Do I got 30 dollars? He can only buy a half-ounce? She comes in and gets half of what we *just bought?*

Bond sits down in a chair next to a small, dirty table. It looks like it started on the inside of the house, possibly as coffee or end table before it ended up outside. He pulls out another quarter-ounce bag of weed and a pack of rollups and starts packing a blunt.

"You stayin to smoke?" Sharmel asks Nikki. Sharmel and I select our dirty seats and pull them close to the dirty table.

"Nah, girl, I'm goin' to a show," Nikki replies with a smirk.

Bond shakes his head. "I don't know how you can sleep after watchin' shit like that," he says.

Shit like what? I know better than to ask while

she is here.

"You a sensitive ass somebody," she scoffs. "I'ma sleep like a baby after I make this money. And you gon' want some."

"Whatever, man." Bond's final lick closes the blunt. He grabs a lighter to seal it.

A few minutes later, Nikki leaves, just like she said she would. She didn't seem to trip at all that I was there or that my presence makes this a couples' setup. Hey, she said she was done with him. That makes my task this evening that much easier.

Dinko goes in the house, and this is probably a good time to ask about Nikki.

"Sooo," I begin, "What kinda show is Nikki goin' to where she gon' make money but not be able to sleep?"

Bond sucks his teeth in disgust. "Man, she into that dog fightin' shit."

"Huh?" Maybe I misheard. "Actual dog fighting?"

I knew Nikki was a wretched fucking miscreant. Told you.

"She do make money, though," Sharmel interjects.

And then while Bond rolls a second blunt, she gives me the brief recap of how Nikki gave Bond and Dinko the money to get that "In Da Air" song produced in a real recording studio so it could be a single.

Well, shit, that explains some things.

Sharmel stops abruptly when Dinko emerges from the back door with a laptop, which he sets on the table. Bond lights one while Dinko pulls up a hip hop video from the 90s on the laptop. Then he pulls up a seat right next to me.

Come collect my soul. Nikki *who*, now?

The smell of his hair oil is mixing with the smell of his deodorant and his sweat. I am tingling. I could straddle him right now.

Dinko and Bond are playing a game of who can play the best old school videos. I would think Dinko would win because he is older, but Bond gets the best of him. Ice Cube's "Steady Mobbin'" put him in the lead for sure. After a while, Sharmel and I get in on the game. I, of course, mop the floor with them all and go even further back. I may not have gone to a lot of parties, but one thing I did do was watch a lot of music videos once we got cable.

After the first blunt is done, I am feeling pretty confident that I can get him to take me inside the house to his room.

When it's my turn to pick a video, I hit them with Nikki D's "Daddy's Little Girl" and am then overcome with the dumbest feeling. Some weed actually does its job and relaxes you, some makes you paranoid, some makes you creative, and some makes you emotional. I am feeling so emotional that I start thinking about my mother. If I stay out all night, she will swear she couldn't sleep because she was worried, or she'll hit me with another one of her other guilt trips.

    Me texting Marshawn: I won't be home tonight.
    Marshawn: Ok.

As the night progresses, I learn a little bit more about Dinko. I had already gathered that he was Bond's cousin, but he is not native to this neighborhood or to this state. Bond was already living here with his three brothers and his father when Dinko moved in last year. I am really interested in what their living arrangements are because I know somebody has to be sharing a room. This house ain't that big. I'll be damned if I'm gettin' hit from the back while some other dude is on the next twin bed over playing Angry Birds.

Meanwhile, Sharmel is walking in and out of the house like this is her second home. Shit, lucky for me, I got hotel money. *Thanks, Silas.*

"My mouth is dry as hell," I say. "What'chall got to drink?"

Sharmel gets up, goes in the house, and comes back with a lukewarm off-brand orange soda. Ew. I use the bottom of my shirt to wipe off the top of the can before popping it open to sip. I'm guessing some liquor is out of the question. That's cool though; I need to be right-minded enough to drive to the *ho-tell.*

I'm thinking about how I can get him out of here and into my car. As with every other man I've ever known, flattery and interest in their hobbies is a good start. I lure with, "So when is y'all next show?"

Bond sneaks a glance at Dinko who merely pulls a freshly lit blunt and stares forward. I look at Sharmel, who is cueing up the next song. She gives me a quick look that tells me the situation is complicated.

"We gotta let shit cool off first," Bond admits. "Somebody saw the van and—"

Dinko cuts him off. "Ay man, loose lips sink ships." He passes the blunt to me.

"I get it," I nod. I take a hit before continuing.

"Sorry for asking. Y'all were just so good. Like, way better than everybody else."

"Thanks," mutters Bond. His cell phone rings. He picks up the phone and looks at the number, frowning. "I don't know who the fuck that is."

Sharmel looks at him quizzically. He doesn't look at her back. Uh oh, I've been there. When they act like they don't know whose number it is. Lord have mercy, I don't need them in a couples squabble that's going to blow my high and my night with Dinko.

Bond's phone rings again. He looks at it, this time with more concern. Then his phone makes another sound, which is probably a text coming in.

"Who is that?" Sharmel asks.

"I don't know," Bond murmurs with a furrowed brow, staring at the text he just got.

I'm about to pass the blunt to him when Sharmel jumps up from her seat and grabs his phone from his hands in one smooth, quick ass motion. She runs toward the front of the house yelling, "I'ma call this number!"

He stands up and follows her but isn't rushing at all. He shouts, "Call it! Tell me who it is!"

Dinko sucks his teeth and leans over to take the blunt back from me. Past their shouting, I hear other random hood noises, like a car racing up the street. I see headlights, and I swear, if Nikki is back, I just fucking give up. That is not how this night was supposed to go. I guess when we do get around to it, this will be a one-night thing instead of a summer fling because I am not fighting her linebacker looking ass.

Gunshots are loud, popping, like right up on us. Sharmel is screaming.

Dinko and I dive to the ground, and I hear a car door slam, then a car speed away, tires screeching. We don't get up immediately, and I am guessing he is being just as cautious as I am in case the coast is not clear.

When Sharmel keeps screaming and we hear two other people come out of the front door of the house yelling, we get up and run to the front.

Bond is lying on the ground, shot.

The two other people out here frantic and telling Bond to "Stay with us!" are Bond's brother and father. They argue briefly about calling the ambulance or taking him to the hospital before they all jump in the car in the driveway and take him. I am left standing here alone.

I walk around to the back yard, find the unfinished blunt in the patchy grass beside the table, grab the bag of weed, get in my car, and go right back to Marshawn's house. I'm fucking traumatized.

♪ ♪ ♪

I can't park in my usual space because Junior Stave's truck is there.

I come in the door, and I can't tell Marshawn what happened because her feet are in Junior's lap.

New Birth is blaring through the living room stereo speakers with the final fuck-you for the night.
♪ *But in my silent nights, I long to hold you tight. It's you I really need. You for me and me for you.*

13

College classes felt like a waste of time after I started dating Bradford. By the end of November 1995, right before I went back home for Thanksgiving break, I asked him if he would marry me and take care of me if I dropped out. He encouraged me to finish college and to wait at least until I was 30 to think about marriage.

It didn't make sense to me at the time. My mother knew that my father was the love of her life when she was 18. Why couldn't I have had that kind of luck? And who the hell would want to wait until 30 for marriage? He turned out to be right, of course. I told him my parents' story and he was highly entertained by it. He even asked me more about it several times.

Bradford and I were able to steal a few hours here and there when he wasn't working. We mostly went out to some basic dinners, followed by basic hotels. I asked him why he wasn't keeping up with the same level of hotel and dinner he did that first night. He explained it the same way he talked about most things, with little insights that I think about to this day. Save special things for special occasions; Appreciate the beauty in life's ordinary things; and All we have is the present.

He didn't seem to have much time for me after I asked him about marrying me. But that was okay because I still had my little crush on Courtney. I had already pulled Courtney into college campus life and into the idea of being my first. I mean, I hadn't invited him to be my first like I had invited Akil. I just planted the idea because, as with everything else with him, I enjoyed reeling him in.

I didn't see a lot of Courtney outside of class during my first three weeks with Bradford. But as soon as December rolled in and Bradford became so busy, the timing turned out to be just right.

There was some kind of Christmas/Kwanzaa show on campus on December 9th, in time for the campus folks to get in a good holiday celebration together before packing up for the break. Courtney mentioned it in class and was so excited about his own hand in its production that most of our class decided to attend. The show was a huge success, standing room only, and Courtney was part of the well-produced closing number. He and a few other guys sang the Temptations' version of "Silent Night," which led into a whole choir performance of Donny Hathaway's "This Christmas."

I guess Courtney's falsetto made a lot of panties wet that night, because after the show, more girls were flocking about than usual. He looked shy and embarrassed—even though I know he must have loved it—but I decided I was going to save him from the ruckus. I ran up on him like there was some emergency he needed to tend to backstage, then led him straight out the back door of the auditorium.

"We going to your place?" I beckoned him with

my eyes and whole vibe. He knew what was up.

He hesitated briefly because that was the right thing to do, then I felt his whole demeanor change to *Fuck it*. All those girls fawning over him had opened the door for me to slide into place.

We pulled up to a house about five minutes away from campus. He parked on the street and led me around to a side door that opened to a basement. Inside, there was a living room, kitchenette, and a bedroom with a bathroom attached. The walls were decorated with posters of jazz musicians and old Blaxploitation movies.

Given that theme, I couldn't wait to see what music he would play to set the mood. It turned out to be Mary J. Blige's *My Life* album. Didn't match the theme I was expecting, but I could dig it.

"You smoke?" he asked, plopping down on his couch.

My man.

I took off my coat and was immediately disappointed in his choice to spark up some half-a-jay he pulled from the side table instead of rolling a fresh one. It was all I needed, though; Mary J Blige was doing the rest of the work.

♪ *Oooh there's work to do. I wanna get real close to you, I wanna get you in the mood.* Of course, Courtney's nervous ass took the first two pulls, but I had a plan for when he passed it to me. I took my first pull, and then instead of taking a second, I put the lit end in between my teeth and leaned forward to his mouth. He opened his mouth, and I blew, blasting the smoke directly in. Of all the things I learned from Akil, the *shotgun* was one of the most fun. I let him sit back and cough it out while I took another two pulls. ♪ *Just relax, and I'll take care of you.* I stubbed out the joint and straddled him, not wanting to risk the possibility of him changing his mind.

I kissed him slowly, a few simple lip-to-lips. I teased him like this until he thrust his tongue into my mouth. Of all the things I learned from Bradford, the tease was one of the most fun—and the most useful. ♪ *Give me all your love and don't stop, my love's waiting when you reach the top.* We kissed as if we were hungry for each other, like we had been waiting for this moment all semester, like it was our secret.

"I don't want to hurt you," he breathed. Between kisses, he whispered, "Just show me what to do... we can take it slow."

He still thought I was a virgin. I couldn't let that go to waste, now could I?

I pulled off my top. He clutched my breasts in his hands, and then went at them ravenously with his mouth. He didn't even bother unhooking my bra; he just pulled titties out of cups and went to work. Bradford had broken me out of being self-conscious about my body, so I hopped off him to take off my jeans, and then got right back on top of him to keep kissing him.

I had three weeks of practice being tortured by the wait, so I let him get to the point where he practically tore my panties off. He flipped me from his lap onto the seat of the sofa. Positioning himself between my legs, he went straight for the bullseye with his mouth. Well, with the tip of his tongue. ♪ *I gave my heart to you, what more can I do to show you how much I care?* Where I was thinking Bradford must have taken a course in making me orgasm with his mouth, I wondered if Courtney had ever attempted anything like this before. He was doing these little licks and some side-to side, very light pressure stuff. As hot as he had gotten me with the kisses, he damn near lost me with the terrible oral. ♪ *But see, all I ask, that you make me feel like I'm somebody.*

"Let's go in your room," I panted.

He picked me up to carry me to his room while my legs were wrapped around his waist. The demonstration of strength earned him back a few points. In his room, the cheap mattress bounced double-time as he practically threw me onto the bed in a rush to take off his clothes. I finally unhooked my bra, and he hurried under the covers.

He started kissing me again, and I was looking forward to feeling him get hard, but I couldn't feel anything in that area. After a few more minutes, he reached onto his nightstand for a condom with no brand name, then put it on under the covers.

He groaned. "Let's take it slow," he said, getting into position to enter me. After I felt a poke or two, he asked, "Is it in?"

"I don't know," I said.

He did some fumbling down there, but I was still playing shy virgin, so I wasn't going to help him out. I felt something go in but barely.

"Is it in?" he asked, getting annoyed.

"I don't know," I answered.

I was getting annoyed. I couldn't even hear Mary J anymore.

He started moving. And then he stopped. And reached down again.

I felt a poke. "What are you doing?" I asked.

"Tighten up," he complained. "I thought you said you were a virgin." He looked into my face as if that were a lie.

"I am!" I insisted. "Are you sure you're even in?"

He lifted up my left leg and tried going at it harder. I don't know if he never got hard or was just that small. After a few seconds, he gave up.

Like, at 28, you would know you had a little dick by then, right? So, he should have known how to maneuver it?

He rolled off me, defeated. "Let's just try this another time. I'm tired."

"Okay." I was so ready to get out of there. "Do you want to take me back to campus?"

"I can call you a cab." And he did.

Do you know how many years it took before I could listen to the *My Life* album again?

When I arrived back to campus, Bradford was waiting for me in the lobby of my dorm. He was wearing a suit and his badge was big and shiny around his neck.

A few passersby were whispering, and the girls on front desk duty were looking at me like they couldn't wait to activate the rumor mill.

As soon as he saw me, he got up and motioned for me to go back outside. "Keep walking," he instructed me, once we were out of the dorm's front door. "Come on."

I followed him to an unfamiliar car with darkly

tinted windows. He did his usual gentlemanly thing, putting me in the passenger side before going to the driver's side.

"Why did you do that?" I demanded. "Now everybody's going to be thinking the worst!"

"Fuck them. Who were you with tonight?" He was calm and his voice was quiet.

"Excuse me?"

"Don't stall. Who was it?"

"It was a friend of mine." I couldn't believe he was jealous, but after the night I had with Courtney, I was glad to see him.

"What's his name?" He was eerily calm.

I hesitated.

"What's his name?" He asked again, so calm and sad looking, as if I had broken his heart.

"Courtney. But it's nothing. Trust me. Nothing at all."

"Courtney who?"

14

Marshawn

Roshawn wasn't back in school for her second semester of college a whole month before I had a whole new slew of reasons to worry about her. In early February, the weekend before Valentine's Day, Ro and Kaia came home for a visit. That was the first surprise—I wasn't used to Ro coming home with Kaia on a weekend. But Kaia's big brother Kai had bought her a little piece of car for Christmas, and I was feeling glad that I didn't have to keep picking the girls up or arranging transportation for them anymore.

That Saturday, they said they were going to the mall, and I heard them whispering about Valentine's Day presents. Kaia had a crush that she said wasn't serious. I don't know what Ro would have needed with a present, because she said she wasn't seeing the professor or Prince Akeem anymore, and she hadn't mentioned anyone else. Then again, she never mentioned the professor either until she was pregnant.

While they were out, a police detective showed up at the house. He said he needed to question Ro about some drug dealer who shot somebody. He knew all about Ro and showed me detailed notes from a time he had questioned her before.

I did not send her to college to get pregnant. I did not send her to college to be involved with a drug dealer. For all I did to keep her away from street mischief, as soon as she was out of my sight, she ran straight toward it.

I had already set Roshawn up with a bank account that I regularly put money in—not too much, but enough where she wouldn't want for little things like paying for her own food if she went out, buying an outfit or two once a month, getting what she needed from a drug store, things like that. There was no need for her to be involved with some drug dealer. That's just greed at that point. Stupidity and greed are a dangerous combination.

When they got back from the mall, I went the fuck off. I asked her about this whole situation with the drug dealer, and she acted more angry than ashamed that the detective had come to the house. She told me it was Prince Akeem who was selling weed and that she hadn't seen him since she was questioned. I tried to make her call the detective in front of me, but she refused.

I was two seconds from knocking her ass out, but figured I needed her to trust me if I was going to get any information about her life. That was what I had been regretting about her turning 18. I mean, I was glad she was alive, but I knew there wouldn't be much I could do to protect her. She would make her own decisions, and I would just have to be there when she fell.

At the end of the spring semester, she told me

that she wasn't going back to school. I was crushed. Pregnant, hanging out with drug dealers, dropping out of college. That was not how her life was supposed to go.

15

I was already trying to get the fuck up out of Marshawn's house, but I need to be GONE. NOW.

Junior, how? Like, what? That's just gross. It is sick.

I stayed the night here last night because I was doubly traumatized and couldn't think straight, much less drive.

Now I have to swallow my pride and hit Silas again, even though he never responded yesterday when I said I was getting a hotel room.

> Me: Can you suggest a hotel with a reasonable, modest price?

It takes twenty minutes for him to get back to me.

> Silas: Is it really that bad?
> Me: You have no idea. I will tell you about it when I see you.
> Silas: Come to my hotel for now. You remember where it is?

Jackpot.

Me: Yes. Which room?

I pack a whole week's worth of stuff and debate myself about whether to take the weed with me. I settle on just the partly-smoked blunt, since Silas doesn't smoke. I'm sure I will be glad I left myself something when I get back to get all of my stuff.

When I leave, Marshawn is upstairs in her room. At least Junior had the class to leave shortly after I got back last night.

♪ ♪ ♪

Silas' room is actually a suite, and it looks very lived in. After I sit my bag down, he offers me a seat on the sofa by holding his hand out toward it.

"How long have you been here?" I inquire.

"About two months." He looks embarrassed—an emotion I would have never expected to see on him.

I look down at his now empty ring finger. "So, you *are* getting a divorce?"

"Yep." He grabs the remote and turns down the tv. "So, what happened?"

Now it's my turn to be embarrassed. I open my mouth but can't say anything. All I can do is shake my head.

"I wasn't tryna drink today," he says. "But here you go, lookin' like you need a drink."

"I may be too mad to drink," I pout.

"I hear that. I been there."

"My mother," I begin slowly, because I cannot believe I am saying this out loud, "is ... fucking ... I guess ... Junior."

"JUNIOR WHO?" he bellows.

"Junior...Stave."

His mouth hangs open as he blinks. "How in the..." he starts.

I cut him off. "Just ... sit with this, with me, for a minute, okay? It's all I have right now. I cannot go any further at this time."

He sits back against the sofa and folds his arms. I can practically see gears turning in his head as he tries to make sense of what I just told him.

"Nah, man, I need a drink." He leaps to his feet and walks to the kitchen area.

Marshawn got her demand met. I was in no mood for alcohol.

16

Looking back on my first year of college, maybe I simply wanted the drama of getting pregnant. Everyone close to me—Kaia, my mother, and Bradford—told me to get on birth control pills. I took my time doing what I needed to do, and lucky me. I never wanted to have Bradford's baby, though. I thought I was ready for a grownup relationship, but not motherhood. Fortunately, he supported my decision to end the pregnancy.

When I got back to school in January 1996 after the winter break, I didn't see Courtney on campus at all. A few of his student fans were concerned that he quit abruptly. Rumors circulated about a scandal with a student, but no one could confirm anything. He was just gone.

Things with Bradford got worse quickly. I didn't feel the same way about him as I did when I was dumb enough to ask him about marrying me. First, it was my concerns over him having something to do with Courtney's sudden departure, then it was because he had the nerve to go to my house and talk to my mother about that thing with Akil. And then, he didn't return my calls or messages for a week after that.

When I was finally able to confront him, he told me that he was worried that I had been seeing other people and that going to my mother was his way of getting the truth. If all of that weren't enough, I still wouldn't hear from him for days at a time. It drove me nuts.

As much as I wanted to play grownup, it's not like Bradford took me around his friends and family or asked me to live with him. All I could do was wait for him to be available. Eventually, I felt like enough of a fool to stand up for myself and make the decision to move on from him.

It was hard, though. I really felt like I loved him. He made me feel beautiful—other than the fact that he was obviously hiding me. After one of his disappearing acts that April, I broke it off with him. We had a heated argument, the only time he ever raised his voice to me, but I couldn't take it anymore. The whole range of emotions took its toll, and living on campus and going to classes became hell. Next thing I know, I was moving back home.

Marshawn was acting angry that I was depressed. I didn't get any empathy from her at all, just bitching about where she went wrong, how if I had a job I wouldn't sit around eating all day, and how I wasn't like her or my father because they were strong and I was too spoiled. I didn't tell her about Bradford because that would have been one more thing in her arsenal.

It took me another few months to get out of bed and get a job working at a drugstore. On my 19th birthday, I was working, and who walks in the store but Bradford. He had gotten a promotion and somehow even better looking.

I was still deep in the throes of depression, having altered my life path to working in a drugstore and residing with my mother instead of living the life of a wild and carefree college student. I felt like a ball of self-pity and flab.

Bradford looked at me like I hadn't changed a bit. "Damn, I missed you." He smiled at me with his full, smooth, pillowy lips and a mischievous sparkle in his brown eyes.

I called Marshawn and told her I was going to a club with my coworkers.

I had gotten used to him playing it cool, or merely being cooler than me because he just was. But at dinner that night, he was romantic, charming, funny, and lighter in spirit than I remembered. We talked like old friends. When I attempted to order only a salad, he ordered me shrimp scampi with angel hair pasta. "Don't be changing up on me now," he comforted.

As soon as we got into the hotel room, he had me up against the wall, kissing me like he really, really missed me. Once he knew I was his for sure, he led me to the bed, laid me on it, and kept kissing me. He let me be the one to stop for us to take off our clothes. Once we were both naked, he laid on his back and pulled me on top of him. He sensed my hesitation and said, "You're beautiful, baby. Mine no matter what." I showed my appreciation by exploring a lot of new moves. By the time he was about to come, he was moaning, "Tell me... tell me..."

"I belong to you ... I belong to you." I came too.

The next morning, he took me to breakfast and

shopping, even bought me lingerie. We discussed the fact that it was time for me to get my driver's license because I had been taking cabs to and from work, sometimes catching rides with coworkers or my mother.

"I'll see you soon. Get your license so we can work on getting you a car." He dropped me off at home and kissed me before I got out of the car.

I didn't see Marshawn standing at the front door. I wasn't paying attention because her car wasn't on the parking pad.

She let me get inside before she started. "Who the fuck was that?"

"Nobody," I answered. I couldn't let her blow my high. Other than weed, the only thing that ever made me high was Bradford.

"WHO WAS IT?" she yelled.

I stayed calm. "Why are you doing this? I'm not 16. I'm 19."

"I know how old you are! I asked who that was!" She got in my face like she was about to hit me.

I thought about what I had just said. I was 19, not 16. And I was high and I didn't care. "His name is Bradford."

She paused and it hit her. "Bradford, the detective who came by here looking for you back in February?!"

"Yep."

"Are you crazy? What the fuck is wrong with you?" As she stood there dumbfounded, I walked past her to my room. She was on my heels. "The detective? And before, it was the professor! What ... why ..." She couldn't even get a question out.

I sat on my bed and looked at her with pity.

"This is dangerous!" she declared. "You can't do this!"

Still calm, I asked, "How did I know you would say that I can't date an older man, even though you did?"

"Why do you want to do what I did? I have been trying your whole life to get you away from what I did! I want you to finish college! I don't want you to have kids early! I want you to live a good life and have a career! I want you to be able to take care of yourself!" She was so frantic that I thought she was going to have a nervous breakdown or a heart attack from all of her overexcitement.

"Ma, all you do is work and brag about how strong you are because you did it all yourself. That's not what I want to do! I want to have someone, a man I can count on, to be with me. I want to marry a rich man so I don't have to work as hard. Who wouldn't want that?"

"You can't count on no man! What makes you think a woman can EVER count on a MAN?" She had me there. "You can't decide whether you want to be grown or be taken care of. They not the same thing, sweetheart." She was no longer yelling, but she hadn't relaxed so much as she had resigned to the fact that I was just too dumb to get it.

Sitting down on my bed, she contemplated for a few moments. The next things she told me were both a shock and a relief.

She filled in some details about my grandfather's businesses and money, about my father's money, what was now her money, and what would one day be MY money. She didn't give me dollar-amount details, but assured me that she had to work, first, for her own dignity, and second, for appearances. If she had just sat back and lived off of the money she was left with, she disclosed, there would be too many questions and too much sniffing around. It would also eventually run out given the lifestyle to which we were accustomed, which was relatively modest.

According to her, a good number of people, from the police to everyday hustlers to distant family members, had long suspected that she had access to my grandfather's and my father's money. It had even been another source of distrust between her and my grandmother.

"We have to work, still," she explained. "The money ain't gonna last us forever if we ain't addin' to it. So, since you *have* to work, you may as well get a job you like. A job where you can use your brain. Not everybody can do that. Make sure you can take care of yourself. You have me while you have me, but even I'm not promised to you forever."

With that, I cried. She pulled me in for a hug and I let the tears flow for a few minutes. When I was done and blowing my nose, she said, "I don't trust that detective. For all I know, he is sniffing after my money. OUR MONEY."

"Ma, I need my driver's license."

"You sure do," she said.

Bradford never came back to the drugstore, but he periodically left me messages through my pager's voicemail. I never called him back. Marshawn's money bombshell had hit me and I started thinking about how interested he was in my parents' story.

Eventually, I got my license, and my mother bought me a used Toyota Tercel. In the meantime, Thomas, the man who would become my stepfather, was spending more and more time at the house with her. When she told me they wanted to get married, we both decided that I should move out.

I chose to move to Atlanta, where so many others were also headed, in order to get the full effect of taking care of myself—with a new, very small money cushion.

17

Marshawn

Junior is my friend, okay? He is really sweet, and at 38 years old, he is a grown ass man. Every time I think Roshawn is finally growing up, she shows me that there are still so many things that she doesn't understand. She will learn, though.

At some points in our lives, we don't have a choice in the lessons we learn. They just pop up and we deal with them.

And anyway, she said she wasn't coming home that night. Shit, I tried to be discreet.

I asked her and Junior several times if they were dating. They were both adamant—separately and independently of each other—that they were just friends and had no intentions of dating and/or sex.

Junior and I haven't even kissed, but we are thoroughly enjoying each other's company. She can get back to chasing Deebo or Mandingo or whoever with the dreadlocks and let me mind my business. When you get to be a woman in your fifties and a man in his thirties just wants to hang out, bring you food, bring you something to drink, talk some gossip, and practice his reflexology skills, holla at me.

Another thing she doesn't know yet is that Thomas and I have gotten what we needed out of our arrangement, and we are officially divorced. No one else knows this except for my brother Marcel and Ro's Aunt Zelda.

The arrangement between Thomas and me was none of Roshawn's business back when we got married. After I found out that her dumb ass was fucking that detective, I knew I was going to have to intervene. I couldn't do anything too blatant because that would have driven her closer to him, but I wasn't going to sit back and let this dude ruin her life trying to get at my money. I spoke to my mother and Zelda about it, and we enlisted some help from connections we had in law breaking *and* law enforcement. One road led to Thomas, an old friend of the family who moved away to New York with Marcel a long time ago.

Thomas has always been the type they call an enforcer. Even though he and Marcel had to move to where they could live their best lives, he was always someone to be counted on to handle business, so he stayed on call. Something came up with him where he needed to be married—to a woman—to protect certain benefits and upward mobility, so we made a deal. We made a deal just in time for me to need some help getting Detective Bradford Wallace away from my daughter.

Please understand that in some lines of work, giving a lot of detail is not an option. For my own freedom and safety, there is a lot I do not know and a lot I do not want to know. What I can tell you, though, is that a few months after Ro's 19th birthday, Detective Wallace had a little situation with an officer-involved shooting and had to move away. He was no longer within a 200-mile radius of my daughter.

18

Michelle, a girl who lived on my same floor my first semester in college was already living in Atlanta when I got there in 1997. Kaia was surprised at my new life—not that I had dropped out of college, but that I moved to a new, big city. She is the one who got me in touch with Michelle.

Michelle was working for a small promotions company run by four men that hired models to go to parties, sometimes provide bottle service, but mostly to guarantee that a party had enough pretty women there. They had a high turnover rate, she explained, so every few months, they held an audition or "model call" where young women would go and apply to be on the promotions team. Michelle was really cute, had that fun, down-for-whatever personality, and always kept her braids looking fresh. I knew from freshman year that her real hair was rather unfortunate, but once she discovered long braided styles, the men discovered her. She convinced me that I was "cute enough" (her words) to get a job being paid $75 per party by just showing up, chatting up men, dancing with them, and sometimes bringing out drinks or champagne.

I went to the model call on a Wednesday evening after I had been in town for about three weeks and hadn't come across anything else I wanted to do. It was December, and I wanted to be able to buy Christmas presents for my mother, Kaia, and Auntie Zee with money I had earned instead of with the money that was placed into my account. A job as a secretary or an administrative assistant would have been my next try-for if the party model thing didn't work out.

I spent the entire day at the mall with Michelle picking out an outfit that would boost my qualifications. We decided it would be best to accentuate my butt, which she said was my best feature. I ended up with a halter-neck gold dress that she swore set off my skin tone, made to be tight in the back but loosely draped and ruched in the front. It did a magnificent job of masking my un-flat stomach.

Michelle accompanied me to the audition at a night club whose happy hour was just kicking off. I followed her to a room on the second level, where there were the four men who ran the promotions company, some girls who were already on the party team, and about fifteen hopefuls like me. We hopefuls were in our finest club gear, but it was obvious who spent money and who was working with the wear-once-and-throw-away variety of clothes and accessories. I landed right in the middle. The girls who were already on the team wore variations of black spandex mini dresses. They stood by the bar, a few feet from the men, with folded arms and straight faces.

The men sat at the bar and made a show of ordering drinks before turning around on their stools to give their attention to the women waiting to be chosen. They were all dressed as if some local designer had given them free clothes—a lot of experimental drawstrings, pockets, and random stripes.

"A'ight, start the music!" one of them called to a DJ in a corner booth.

The speaker system blasted the opening notes of the "In My Bed (So So Def Remix)" by Dru Hill. When Jermaine Dupri said, *You wanna dance? I'ma make you dance*, another of the men commanded, "Dance, ladies!"

"Come on, ladies, dance! We need to see you dance!" the first one instructed.

A few of the young women started dancing right away, like they didn't have to be told twice. The rest of us got into a reluctant groove and then tried to act like we meant it when we remembered the whole scene was essentially a competition. I was mentally eliminating girls as I did my best sexy moves.

Man, I'm telling you, if Michelle hadn't smoked me out while we were getting dressed and made me take a shot of Absolut before I walked up in there, I would not have been able to keep dancing. A third of the girls went full stripper mode, a third were either off beat or just couldn't really dance that well, and I was in the other third, attempting to dance, stay cute, *and* keep my dignity. The young women who were already on the team studied us like they were going to be asked their opinions.

"Oh nah, you gon' have to come harder than that!" shouted one man.

"Ain't no poles here, sweetheart, wrong audition!" laughed another.

I did my best to mostly keep my butt toward the men as I gave them other various angles of my movement. The DJ mixed into "It's All About the Benjamins," which was a lot easier to dance to. The men started eliminating shortly thereafter.

"In the green, thanks for comin', that's all," the loudest of the men yelled over the music.

"Shorty in the black dress... nah, the short one... nah, the other short one... thanks for coming, good night."

"Girl in the white, yo, it's December, what'chu doin? God bless, thanks for comin'."

They kept eliminating until there were seven of us left. These were all of the girls I had sized up as the ones most likely to be chosen. Even the ones without the supposed ideal body shape were at least pretty enough that a guy would look twice. Two of them couldn't dance too well, though. Michelle walked over to one of the men and whispered something to him.

"We only need four," he responded, loud enough for everyone else to hear.

"She ain't got no ass, man," I heard another one of the men say.

"Nah, she got a little bit of flavor though," another replied as The DJ mixed into "Crush on You" by Lil' Kim and Lil' Cease.

"That one got enough ass for all of them," he added, and I assumed he meant me. "She type ordinary though."

Ordinary: the story of my life. I decided that if I was going to go through this kind of bullshit to be down with their team, and very possibly *not* get chosen,

I was going to go out in an *extra*ordinary way.

I turned toward the men so I could properly size them up, and by the time Lil' Kim's first verse started, I had done the choosing. I picked out the one who looked to be the second most intelligent among them, who was also the third best looking. He was about 5'9, stocky, and had the kind of head shape that kept him in baseball hats to maintain a modicum of panache.

♪ *Ay yo shorty, won't you go get a bag of the lethal.* I walked directly up to the dude, maintaining the beat to the music and eye contact with only him. When I got to him, I danced and rapped along, specifically to him and for him. ♪ *The only one thing I wanna do is freak you.* I blew dude's ego all the way up. By the time Lil' Kim and I asked, *Shall I proceed?* All four men were hyping me up, shouting, *Yes, indeed!* By the end of the verse, I had secured the first spot offered.

After the second party I worked, Kenny, the victim of my fake seduction at the audition, asked me out to a late-night-early-morning breakfast. He asked when no one else was around because, as he explained at breakfast, he didn't want the other folks on the team to know. It seemed to me like a very open secret that the guys tried their luck with various girls on the team. Michelle had already bagged the best looking of the foursome, and as with everything else in life, the people who fared better in this atmosphere were the ones who could keep their emotions out of simple things like sex.

I worked two or three parties per week, and while it was unfulfilling, I still had visions of marrying one of the athletes or other famous people at the parties we were working.

I told Marshawn all about it, and she didn't understand, first of all, how that was an actual job, and second, why I would do it for so little money. She was hoping I could do something "more stable, with some benefits" as she put it. I did tell her that I was seeing Kenny, and that he would regularly give me money that amounted to about $100 to $200 a week. The hypocrisy was amazing on her part—like, Bradford apparently only wanted me for my money, and Kenny was supposedly controlling because he was giving me money. I knew then that I would never win with her unless I was in a lonely ass marriage like she was, with some boring dude with whom I would only ever have money in common.

Kenny wasn't a bad guy at all. He was 29 and really did his best, but it was frustrating to find myself in yet another relationship where we had to hide it from everyone we knew. At least I had sense enough this time around to get on birth control pills, but it seemed like it controlled birth by making me irritable and never in the mood to do anything sexual. A month into dating Kenny, I picked up on the pattern that he was giving me money to put me in the mood, and that my sex with him was pretty much a thank-you.

I could have met more men at the parties we worked, but any time I was close to getting someone's phone number, he would block immediately. Even when men handed me their business cards, he would wait until the end of the night and politely ask me to give him the cards; he always knew exactly how many. While he insisted that we "keep everyone else out of our relationship," they all knew we were a thing because of how closely he watched me and how he always ended up beside me when we were all together.

They used between 10 to 20 girls per party, depending on the venue size, and there was a core eight who were always around. Sometimes the guys did parties that I wasn't invited to work at, and I would hear later that they wanted "the exotic ones" or "the skinny ones" or "the pretty ones." Under Michelle's urging, I got a haircut. I had always regarded the trendy short styles on Nia Long and Halle Berry as too difficult to maintain if you didn't have weekly hairdresser money, but thanks to Kenny, I had weekly hairdresser money.

When the HBCU Spring Break Season of 1998 arrived, we had a slew of parties lined up and even started going out of state to accommodate the demand. There was a professional athlete who was throwing a big bash in his backwoods hometown, and we girls were mad about having to stay four-to-a-room at some low-quality motel there. The guys made up for it by promising us a trip to the beach the day after the party—their treat for food and drinks all day. Michelle and I hit the mall to buy new bathing suits, pajamas, and more variations of the tight black mini dress. The shopping got us hyped about the trip, and I could just feel that something exciting was going to happen.

We knew we were allowed only one drink at parties, so we girls pre-gamed together at the motel before piling into rented SUVs driven by promotions team security. The party turned out to be a lot of fun, and we were presently surprised by the quality and demeanor of the guys from that area. Kenny wasn't so possessive that night. He and the other guys seemed as charmed by the ladies there as we were by the men.

The girls on the team habitually left parties before the lights came on. No lingering and loitering about; once our jobs were done, we were done. We usually either walked out in groups or the guys or their security would walk us to our cars, cabs, friends' or boyfriends' rides. However, for these parties out of town, we would have to wait for the guys to handle their money business because we all rolled together in a caravan. It was usually more carefully controlled, but this night had everyone feeling relaxed. This time, the girls had already gotten in the SUVs, which were pulled up in front of the place. Kenny and Rootie, one of the other guys in charge of the team, were talking to two girls standing outside.

"You gon' get your man, girl?" asked Sheba, the girl sitting to my left in the second row of seats.

"No, I hope he get her number," I chuckled.

"Please," said a girl sitting in the third-row seat behind me. We called her Loosey because she bought them from corner stores. "He stuck to you like glue."

As we all snickered and talked about the party, I saw a familiar figure exit the club and walk up to the women talking to Kenny and Rootie. He said something that I couldn't hear.

"I'm just talkin!" one woman protested to the man who had just walked up.

It was fucking Bradford.

"Yo, homie, you can back the fuck up," warned Rootie. He was not the type to back away from a fight.

But neither was Bradford.

"I ain't talkin' to you," said Bradford, cool and

calm as ever, but still brimming with street swagger.

I jumped out the truck as the girls, the driver, and Kenny yelled at me to stay in the truck.

"Bradford!" I walked up to them.

I didn't think about what I was doing before getting out and approaching, but my gut told me that adding another layer of drama would actually quell potential violence. Also, I wanted Bradford to see me.

You should have seen the look on his face. The cool and calm was gone, and it was like he was looking at a ghost.

"Who the fuck are you?" threatened the woman, stepping toward me.

"Who the fuck is this?" Kenny asked me, looking back and forth between me and Bradford.

Bradford automatically positioned himself to protect me from both of them. He and Kenny turned out to be the same height, but if I hadn't seen them right next to each other, I would have sworn Bradford was taller.

"My fiancé!" the woman yelled directly at me.

"Both of y'all back up!" Bradford ordered.

"Slim, you back the fuck up before we back your ass up!" Rootie roared.

"Who the fuck is she? Who the fuck is she?" The woman kept asking.

Bradford had no choice but to flash his badge to Rootie and Kenny. "I know her."

"And?" Kenny inquired, looking at me for an answer.

I shrugged. "I know him."

"You better tell me something or you can have

this fuckin' ring back!" Bradford's fiancée shoved him.

"Come on, girl," her friend pleaded, holding her back. "Leave his ass. I told you he was cheatin' on you! Come on, let's go!"

"You fuckin' him?!" Kenny yelled at me.

I knew as well as Kenny did, that he watched my every move when I was out working parties, that he regularly showed up unannounced at my apartment, and that he left clothes, shoes, and other items there, making sure they were undisturbed in his absence. He paged me whenever I was out with Michelle, checking to see if I was where I said we were going to be. It was highly unlikely that I was cheating on him, but everyone here could *feel* me and Bradford. Shit, me and Bradford could *feel* me and Bradford.

I rolled my eyes. "You know I'm not."

"I don't believe neither one of y'all!" the fiancée shrieked. "It's over! Fuck you!" She burst into tears and her friend led her away.

Kenny looked like he didn't know what to believe. "Ay yo, get in the truck," he said, rubbing his face hard with both hands. "I'll holla at you later."

Bradford looked at me. "You a'ight?"

"Yes, I'm alright." I had to make sure my face matched my words, so Kenny wouldn't disappear like Courtney had.

"Call me if you need me," he added as I walked back toward the truck.

The next day, Kenny went back to Atlanta instead of going to the beach with us.

By the time, I got back to Atlanta, I had already left my phone number and address on Bradford's voicemail using the number I had for him. He reached my apartment about an hour before Kenny did, and then helped me pack Kenny's stuff in a bag that was waiting for him at the door. When Kenny knocked on the door, Bradford let him in.

"What the fuck is goin' on?" Kenny asked, perplexed.

"How old is she?" Bradford asked Kenny, tilting his head toward me.

"Twenty-two," Kenny replied, looking at me.

"Twenty," revealed Bradford.

Kenny's mouth dropped open.

"She don't work for y'all no more." He bent to pick up the bag of Kenny's stuff. "Leave her alone, man."

Kenny left and Bradford locked the door. "That dude, though?" His voice indicated that he knew I could do better.

"That fiancée though?" I countered as he walked toward me. I was jealous.

"She ain't you." He didn't stop until our bodies were touching. "I thought you didn't want me anymore," he apologized, his eyes holding mine.

I had to look away. I didn't have the words for 'I thought you were after my family's money,' although I didn't care one bit about that in the moment.

He gently lifted my chin so I had to look at him. "You don't want me no more?"

I tried to grab his face to kiss him as an answer.

"No, tell me." Same ol' Bradford.

"I want you," I assured him.

He practically dived into my mouth to kiss me. I had missed him so much, a man who knew how to kiss me, touch me, and fuck me right. After he kissed me passionately for about a minute, he stopped to say, "I have to go back tonight."

I led him back to my bedroom and we laid on top of the bedspread, facing each other. I waited for him to continue, but he just stared at me.

"I like your haircut. That's fly as shit," he said.

When he first saw it, Kenny had only said, "Why you cut your hair?"

I blushed. "So now what?" I asked.

"We gon' find you a job," he replied. "Why don't you go back to school?"

"I'm tired of school."

"Next year, you goin' back to school."

What I was also tired of was men telling me what to do. I sighed and rolled my eyes.

"You gon' leave me again 'cause I want you to go back to school?" he asked.

"What time you gotta go back?" I was not trying to have that conversation.

"Now." He got up to leave, and I didn't protest.

He returned four days later with roses, $1,000 in cash, a new pack of condoms, a bottle of Hpnotiq, two sets of bedsheets and a comforter set. Shortly after he took his shoes off, the doorbell rang with food he had ordered in advance. We changed the bed linens before we ate. He put all of my old sets of bedsheets and my old bedspread in a trash bag and took it straight out to the dumpster.

Over dinner, we did a very shallow catching up, carefully skipping details about our romantic partners. It was the first time he ever mentioned a mother and a brother, with whom he was planning a family vacation that summer.

He talked about having to move to a different police department in a new city and liking it. "I tried to get in touch with you to tell you I got shot."

"What?!" I felt terrible that I had never called him back or even listened to his messages.

He didn't linger for my sympathy, though. "It was a real messed up situation. I'll tell you about it sometime."

He promised that he would use his connections to find me a job in Atlanta or in the city where I went to school and where we met. In the meantime, he said, he would help me out with money, starting with the grand he had just brought to me. I would have loved to rub that in Marshawn's face, but I knew better than to tell her that I was seeing him again.

He kept telling me how good I looked. While we watched tv, he would look over during commercials and tell me how much he missed me. It seemed like he was proving to me—or to himself—that we could just sit and watch tv together.

By the middle of the second show we watched, there was a commotion outside in the parking lot and it sounded like two women were yelling. At first, we shrugged it off as just another day in the hood, but then one of the women called out, "Brad! Brad!"

We both got up and looked out the window. It was the same two women from outside the club a few days prior and a guy standing with them.

"Shit," Brad muttered. At least he turned to look me in the eyes.

"That's your fiancée, huh?" I was almost done being jealous, but there she was again, with the ability to pull him away from me. Adding to my jealousy was anger at him for not managing to keep her ass from my doorstep.

I never thought he was capable of shame, but it was coming off of him like steam. It was his shame that started turning my jealousy and anger into relief. I thought of the way he rolled up on her outside of the club and how Kenny was always up in my face.

"I don't want to deal with this shit, Brad."

After Kenny, I didn't need another man to pick up the slack on trying to control my life. The situation started to feel more and more like a liberation. I wanted to spread my wings.

He threw his head back and sighed.

After he took his time putting on his shoes and grabbed his keys, there was a brief moment where it seemed like we should hug or make a meaningful goodbye. But I refused to look at him. I wanted him to feel bad for this. He walked out to the parking lot, straight to his car, and drove away. The three who came looking for him scrambled, yelling, back to their car and followed him.

19

Silas has decided that he can swallow his pride and move to his father's house until he sorts out his divorce and where he will live next.

"Why didn't you just move there in the first place?" I ask.

Silas shakes his head before answering. "I didn't want to hear him say, 'I told you so.' When I finally told him everything last week, I had to listen to two or three speeches before he agreed that I should move in with him for the time being."

"He warned you about your wife?"

"Everybody warned me about her."

Over the last three days, Silas and I have become friends. We've been like two people sitting on the same ledge ready to jump but talking each other off of it. He has paid for three carryout deliveries, and I have gone out twice to get us breakfast. I even gave him back the rest of the money that he gave me. When he goes back to his father's place tomorrow, I'll stay here for one more night.

"Mm. I know that journey," I empathized.

"Like my father said, I just had to have what I

wanted." He is not the same sure-of-himself Silas I met at the beginning of the summer.

"You are a smart man," I tell him. "But Love is its own thing. The best among us have no defense, really. Except for the straight sociopaths. And then, I think even they get caught up sometimes ..."

He scrolls through pictures on his phone, stops on one, and hands it to me. On the screen is a teenage boy and an adolescent boy that look exactly like Silas and Jason Mercer, and then a sandy-haired, pale boy who looks like he could be one of their friends.

"I didn't want to see this for what it was," he explained. His vulnerability is even more unsettling than his forwardness was.

I am scared to absorb what he is telling me without saying it out loud. It's is obvious that these are his three boys, but one is not biologically his. I guess that was news to him, and it had to be heartbreaking. Poor Silas.

"That shit broke me," he confessed. "I did try to make it work, even after I got the test to confirm, but she was still..." He shook his head instead of continuing his sentence.

"Damn, Silas. I'm sorry." What else can I say? And he still took the time to try and get me a job. And hit me off with some cash. I hand him back his phone.

"So yeah. My dad had a lot to say." He sighs deeply. "I'm sure I have to apologize to you for bein' disrespectful when we first met. I had just moved out and thought the best way to get over it was to get on somebody else."

If this was just a regular cheating situation, I would be happy to help him with the big payback. But in this situation, I want to make sure he is mentally and emotionally okay.

"No need for that." I put my hand on his. "Shit, it was only the ring that kept me away. And look at us now. Besties." My attempt at humor barely registers.

He has a blank stare and his words come out half-muttered. "I can barely remember a week ago. It's like I been existin', but not experiencin' anything. So, forgive me. I was tryna feel somethin', anything other than what I was actually feelin'."

"You can get past this," I insist. "You and your sons. And I'm here for you. You been here for me. Even going through all this, you have been here for me."

He shrugs.

"Thank you." I squeeze his hand and we sit like that for a while, in silence.

♪ ♪ ♪

Monday, the day that Silas and I part ways as roommates, is the same day that Selena Benson finally gets back to me about a job. It takes all of ten minutes for me to coordinate an interview time through email on my Blackberry, and I now have one day to relax at the hotel alone, one day to return to Marshawn's house and prepare, and then the interview the following day.

Silas' advice was to refrain from doing too much planning about a new apartment (and laptop) right now, but to take it one day at a time until the first two paychecks clear and I have something to work with.

Before he left me alone in the suite, he reiterated, "Fuck them. Focus on YOU."

I guess I should text Marshawn proper warning of my return. I clearly cannot control this situation with her seeing Junior, but I can damn sure help any efforts to keep it the fuck away from me.

> Me: I will be back tomorrow.
> Marshawn: Ok.

Hello, partially smoked blunt.

♪ ♪ ♪

I'm good and high when the texts come through.

> Kai: Hey. We lost Bond. He died an hour ago.

And then...

> Junior: FYI, Bond died today.

I've only texted Sharmel once since he got shot to ask how Bond was doing. I feel bad, but I was figuring out my own shit and bonding with Silas. And of course, my next thought is to text him.

> Me: Did you hear about Bond?
> Silas: Yeah, just now.
> Me: It was bad enough that I was right there when it happened. I feel way

worse now. I just figured he would recover.
Silas: I'm sorry you had to be involved in that. If I were you, I would still keep my distance from that whole shit.
Me: I hear you.
Silas: Do you, though?
Me: *rolling my eyes* So anyway, you doing ok?
Silas: Yep, I'm chillin. Get some sleep. Be cool as a cucumber tomorrow when you go back home. Fuck them. Focus on you.
Me: Fuck them. Focus on me.
Silas: And by them, I mean both Junior AND Dinko.
Me: GOOD NIGHT, DAD.
Silas: I could make a daddy joke, but...

Dude, *I* could make a daddy joke.

Me: I hate you.
Silas: Please don't say that. Not even as a joke.
Me: I apologize. I do not like you.
Silas: That's cool. Good night.
Me: Good night.

I like Silas.

> Me to Kai: I am sorry to hear that. How is
> Sharmel?
> Kai: As bad as u would expect.

I gotta text Sharmel. She is a really sweet person, and I feel like this whole thing with the shooting automatically connects us on a deeper level.

> Kai: I heard u were there when it
> happened. Dinko is all fucked up too.

I remember when just hearing Dinko's name would shift my uterus and make my scalp buzz. But now, nothing. I feel a coldness where I once felt burning heat, a thrilling swirl of psychedelic colors, and uncontrollable waterfalls.

> Kai: Are u ok?
> Me: Yeah. It's kinda weird how ok I am. :(
> Kai: That's good.
>
> Me to Sharmel: I am so sorry to hear about
> Bond. You are in my prayers.
> Sharmel: I am so sad I dont know what to do
> Me: (((HUGS))) Celebrate his life. That
> is all we can do. And pray for comfort.
> I can't imagine what you are going
> through.
> Sharmel: What you doin right now
> Me: Chillin but I'm out of town.

```
Sharmel: I was goin to ask you to come get
         me
```

If I wasn't too high to drive, I would go get her.

```
Me: I'm so sorry I can't right now. I'ma
    hit you when I get back home. I know
    you will need a break.
Sharmel: Ok
```

♪♪♪

Checkout time is 11am, and I am getting every minute's worth of my stay this morning. As I did when Silas was here, I got up at 8am, showered, and went out to pick up breakfast at 9. I saved just enough of the blunt for a breakfast bake so I could be unbothered when I walk back through Marshawn's door.

As I double-check everything to make sure I have all my stuff, I see that Silas left a third of a Jameson bottle on the counter by the refrigerator. I'm telling you, I like that dude. It's the last thing I grab to put in my bag, and as I pick it up, I cry a tear or two. Behind the bottle is the money I gave back to him.

Marshawn's fat ass probably ate all the snacks—probably even shared them with Junior's fat ass. I stopped at the store and got some thin Oreos, sour cream and cheddar chips, and Flaming Hot Cheetos, which I know she won't touch with a ten-foot pole, and then Cherry Coke, which she loves.

I get back to Marshawn's while she is at work, thank God. I have a few hours before our impending battle of who can out-judge whose life decisions. In the meantime, I'm on interview prep and County research. I don't plan to pretend I want to do diversity work, but I will insist that the position is a good way for me to contribute my writing and research skills, as well as my interest in policy.

At 2pm, Marshawn arrives home earlier than I was expecting her. Today's drive-up song is Atlantic Starr's "Send For Me." I am still at the computer in the living room. It's just as well. If my laptop were working properly, I would be hiding in my room instead of facing her, woman to woman.

I turn toward the door as she walks through it.

"Hello," she says, the first to be unbothered. "You back for good?" She sits down on the couch and starts unbuckling the straps to her sandals.

"I have a job interview tomorrow, so I'll be here for a while, but I'll be moving out soon enough." I am doing well being unbothered, if I do say so myself.

"Oh, really? Moving out?"

"Yep, out of your hair."

"I told you about all that. I am happy to have you here. I know you grown, but you are still my child, and I will always look out for you. You will always have a home here. Do you understand?"

"I don't like feeling like a child."

She shrugs. "I don't know what to tell you except that you are my child. And that you are welcome here."

I lean back in the desk chair and sigh. How can I make her understand if she insists on not understanding?

"So are you ok after that boy got shot? I heard

you were right there." She must have heard that from Junior, but I am comforted that she is showing concern over how I am feeling.

"No, I was around back. I didn't see it. I heard it."

"I take it nobody talkin' to the police?" she questioned.

"Ain't nobody said nothin' to me about police."

Shit. I hadn't even considered that the police have to be involved. Maybe it's time for me to step out of my own head and see what's going on.

She didn't say it, but the look on her face read, *Roshawn always in some shit.* At least she was keeping it light for now. "So, what's the job interview for?"

"It's on some diversity committee the County is putting together. Silas recommended me for it." It's a good thing I can mention Silas with no shame since we are not having sex. Not right now, anyway.

"Mmph," she grunts. "He good for somethin', huh?"

"He is," I reply confidently. "He is turning out to be a good dude."

"For the record, I tried not to ask … but are you just fuckin' him for a job, or …"

"No no no noooo!" I interrupt. "I am not doing anything but being friends with him!"

"Junior said you been stayin' with him at a hotel."

"Oh my god! Why is Junior in my business?!"

"Junior is in everybody's business. So while he was at it, I told him to find out where you were. And he told me."

"How…? Never mind." Fucking Junior. I can't wait to tell Silas this. "Anyway, I am NOT sleeping with Silas. He is going through a divorce and a pretty bad situation."

Marshawn just looks at me like she is expecting me to be the usual fool sleeping with a married man.

"He found out his youngest child ain't his." Shit, I had to spill it to somebody and it could only be Marshawn. "I seen the pictures. Like it's his two kids and then some biracial child."

Her face goes from judgment to shock and then sympathy.

"We been through a lot of emotions together these past few days. He was living out of the hotel, but just moved to his father's house. I feel so bad for him."

She shakes her head slowly and takes a deep breath. "Well, Junior …"

I cut her off. "I don't wanna hear nothin' 'bout Junior right now. Excuse my French, but that's y'all shit. I gotta focus on this job and gettin' back into school. Is that okay with you?" I don't have an attitude; I am just tired.

"Okay with me." As we reach a draw in the Battle of the Unbothered, she gets up and goes to the kitchen. "You don't cook no more, huh?" she calls.

"What would you like? I will cook whatever you want."

She comes back out of the kitchen and sits at the dining room table. "And I will eat whatever you cook."

20

Marshawn can be alright. Sometimes, I have to admit it to myself. Yesterday, after I made dinner, she took me to buy something nice to wear for the interview. She picked out and bought my whole outfit: a navy blue short-sleeved business dress, beige pumps with a low heel, appropriately sized gold-plated hoop earrings, and a slimming high-waist brief. She even picked me out a new professional work bag to carry.

I wrapped my hair last night and it is falling nicely this morning. Before I left the house, I snapped a picture of myself and texted it to Silas.

> Me: Ready for my interview!
> Silas: Good luck! Emphasize your writing skills.
> Me: Will do. :)

It's 10am and already 85 degrees out here. After I check in at the security desk, I ask for directions to the restroom. I need to mop up some sweat before I sit for an interview where I am sure to sweat even more.

I expected there to be several other people waiting to be interviewed, but no one else was in the waiting area shared by three smaller offices in one large, combined office.

When I walked up to the receptionist's desk, she said, "Roshawn Bell?"

"Yes."

"You can go in." She pointed to the open door to her left.

When I walked in, Miss International herself was sitting on the front edge of her desk. Roy Janowicz is sitting in a chair beside it. They are laughing, and I hope that is a good sign.

"Hello again, Ruhshawn," she smiles.

"Hey Rehshawn," Roy chimes in his bouncy voice.

"Hello," I respond with equal parts cheer and confidence.

I didn't bother to correct them on pronouncing the *Ro* sound in my name. As Marshawn always says, *Just spell it right on my check*. Besides, I hate to hear people enunciate my name if they lack the ability to put the proper soul and funk in it.

"Have a seat." Selena points the folder in her hand to an empty chair in front of her desk. "So you don't mind writing, huh?"

"No, I don't. I've had training in public reports and policy writing."

"Silas passed on the community engagement report you put together for your town," she says. "We can definitely use you on the committee."

"Yeah," adds Roy. "I do not like the writing part of things, and I know a few others who don't either."

"So, what's your availability?" Selena asks. "I know graduate students are pretty busy."

Fuck. I forgot that Silas had presented me as a grad student.

I play it cool, but don't want to lie because I don't want to be caught later. "My priorities are low for the time being. And, I am applying to programs, so that frees me up until next year."

"Oh?" She looks confused.

"Yeah, I am sorry for the confusion. I chose not to start my program this fall. I prefer to work for a while to be sure about which concentration is the best fit."

"Where were you going?" Roy asks.

I named my undergraduate university. "They had a program where you can continue on to get your master's, but I wanna go for my PhD instead."

That is a lie, but they bought it and kept talking to me about the position. It sounds like I'll be sitting in rooms with people who want to talk about diversity and inclusion and then writing reports about those meetings. They lowball me on the salary, but in my quick calculation, it is enough for a good-enough apartment and modest living. I accept, and Roy takes the next hour or so to get me proper documentation, scan my driver's license, and meet two other people on the committee. I start tomorrow.

♪ ♪ ♪

My first week at work is tiring, and not because I had to do any writing or reporting. I had to sit through meetings and meetings and meetings about diversity this and inclusion that. By God's grace, I don't have to participate in, facilitate, or report on any diversity trainings. This committee, so far, seems to be more about goals for various towns, organizations, and miscellaneous localities. I also spend a lot of time on the internet doing research on population statistics. I am sure that I will learn a lot, and like I said in my interview, I'll be able to find my best fit with this policy stuff.

When I walked into this evening's Town Meeting, they all applauded. The mayor and Ms. Stave were especially congratulatory. Later in the meeting, I learned that it was because they started thinking of me as their "inside man," (yes, they used that term) and couldn't wait for me to report back to them about what was going on in County administration.

I thought she was about to introduce the motion to adjourn, but she says, "Next meeting, Mr. Mercer will be back with an update on the county's plan for community policing. Miss Bell's report said that the businesses were concerned about graffiti, loitering, and having proper police presence." The information I was given also included complaints about The Roost, but I didn't include those.

Their praise makes me feel really proud of myself, and I can't wait to tell Marshawn.

"And Mayor Edwards and I have been in contact with the County Council Administrator's Office about that young man who was shot right in our neighborhood," Ms. Stave continued. "They're sending representatives to the funeral tomorrow."

Shit. I forgot about the funeral tomorrow.

"I suggest that we ALL do our best to make it."

She did that thing where she looks around the table, directly into everyone's eyes, to emphasize her point.

I should have known that Bond's shooting—hell, any shooting around here—would not escape the agenda of the Town Council. At least none of them are acting like they know I was there. So far, the only people who know I was there are Sharmel, Dinko, Silas, Kai, and Junior's gossipy ass, because I am sure he is the one who told Marshawn. Bond's father and brother may know, but they may not remember me.

I don't want any more people than that knowing I was there, I don't want to be seen as a source of information for any authorities, and I don't want whoever did it to come looking for me as if I could point them out. My new job and societal position are finally looking up. I am not trying to step backwards or downgrade to 'witness to shooting.'

After the meeting, I stop by Gene's food setup. His food doesn't look as appetizing as Junior's did.

"What up, baby girl?" he greets proudly.

"Nothin' much. How you doin'?"

"I'm doin' good, doin' good. Sellin' these dinners. Man, I sell a lot too! A lotta return customers!"

And they all talk about how the food ain't like Junior's.

"You goin' to the funeral tomorrow?" he asks.

"Yeah, I'm sure I can go into work late or something." I search my purse for my phone to check the text Sharmel sent with the information. I still haven't had time to go see her, but she says that Nikki is being a good source of support.

"Go to work late? The funeral is at 6:00. In the evening."

"Oh shit!" I exclaim, even though that is kind of a relief. "Okay. Man, this new job got me tired."

"Where you work?"

"Workin' for the County now. A committee for diversity." Damn, it feels good to have a respectable job.

"Oh, County, like Silas!" There's almost a glowing lightbulb over Gene's head. "You see him at work?"

"Not yet, he works in a different division." When one of the town council members walks up to get a plate, I make my escape. "A'ight, Gene. See you tomorrow."

♪ ♪ ♪

"So how do you know Silas?" Selena asks out of the blue as I am doing research from a spare office computer.

"We grew up together," I lied. I don't remember Silas at all from back in the day.

She stands there with a cup of coffee and I feel her eyes and brain taking all of me in to pick me apart. "Oh, so in college, you were like a … What do they call it? Adult learner?"

I look up at her and am one second late in softening the expression on my face that says, *And what the fuck about it?*

"Your resume is interesting," she clarified. "You have a lot of good experience. I knew you weren't just some young, wet-behind-the-ears dummy." She seemed unfazed by my mean mug. "So, what's the deal with Silas? Is he single now, or …?"

Of course. It was always about Silas. She peeped that the ring is gone.

"What makes you say that?" I am not answering her questions. He is on *my* shelf for safekeeping.

"His ring has been off for a while." She is trying to see if I am already walking down that road.

My judgmental stare says, *Ho, I can't believe you are so thirsty. I'm a good Christian girl, myself.*

"Just making sure he's okay…" Her tone and the way she let her eyes drift to the right with a head tilt answers me, *You can pass up that dick if you want to, but I'm tryna hop on that thang.* "He said you'd be at that funeral this evening?"

Right. If Ms. Stave has been in touch with the County Council Administrator's Office, Selena would be in on this.

"Yes." I nod, sobered by the fact that I may not be able to keep my name out of it all.

"Okay, good. We can all sit together, then."

The hell we can.

She did that dumb ass thing where she tucks her hair behind both ears even though it was already tucked. "Oh!" she blurted. "You know your committee and the county police are getting together for the community policing goals?"

"Right, I heard."

"Okay, so they're sending trainers for a community liaison unit. Like, they're police, but you'll have to work with them and county police and the prosecutors to get this thing going. It'll probably be the first big task of your committee."

"Oh. Cool." I don't know why she is treating this like hot gossip.

"So, you know, lots of new faces coming through." She wiggles her eyebrows. "New men from, like, every corner of the county."

Good. Her sights are not set squarely on Silas. I can work with that. Thirst buckets can be fun when they aren't after *your* man.

21

Silas texted me at 4:00.

> Silas: We should be there for the family hour at 5:00. Are you in the middle of something?
> Me: Nothing I can't finish tomorrow.
> Silas: Do you need to stop anywhere, or can you follow me directly over there?
> Me: Nah, I'm good. I can follow you.
> Silas: Come to my office and we can walk out together.
> Me: Be there asap.

I am wearing a black dress that Marshawn doesn't wear anymore. She had me try on three, and we decided on this one because it looks the least like something a scandalous side chick would wear. It's not low-cut, but it is doing something magical for my boobs without a display of cleavage.

Fortunately, Selena is not around, and I can make

a quick exit. As I scoop up a handful of things I have printed from the internet, Roy walks in.

"Skipping out early?" Roy shrilled in his popcorn manner.

"Funeral," I answer, putting papers into my new bag.

"You need a notebook," he gawks.

"Yep." I keep shit short with him and Selena. I know that game where they want you to 'be yourself' and then later claim you're unprofessional or use your personal business against you. But I also know that if you don't smile enough, you're angry and scary and difficult to work with. I look up to smile sweetly at him, but he is looking at my boobage. I hold the smile until he snaps out of it a half-second later.

"You want me to find you some notebooks?" he offers.

"That would be great, yes!" I keep my voice steady and let my eyes offer him a millisecond snapshot of sex. I search his eyes with mine, figuring out if he prefers to work with me as a dumb bimbo or a secret dominatrix.

"I-I'll be right back ..." He backs away, jerking his thumb over his shoulder. "There's some in the, uh—"

Secret dominatrix it is. "I'm in a hurry, but tomorrow, I'm coming to look for you. Thank you so much."

"Sure, sure." He puts his hands in his pockets and tries to act like he is not watching me while I walk confidently out the door.

I walk down a floor to Silas' small, basic office.

He gets up from his chair as soon as I walk in. "Why you look like the cat that just swallowed the canary?"

"What?" I have been continually amazed at how well he reads me. Another unsettling Silas thing.

"Let's go," he says, shooting me a skeptical look.

♪ ♪ ♪

By the time we arrive to the funeral home, there are two different news crews on the entrance lawn and the public is already showing up and taking up parking spaces. There are a lot of the same types of young folks I saw at the rapper showcase, none in proper funeral attire. Closer to the entrance are four police cars. Fuck. This shit keeps escalating.

Silas and I are able to park right next to each other. He is ever the gentleman, keeping pace with me as we walk toward the entrance. At this point, I guess we aren't very concerned with appearances, though I have yet to tell him that Junior knew I stayed with him at the hotel.

When we walk into the chapel, I recognize folks from The Roost, the Father's Day cookout, and of course, Bond's father and the brother who was there that night. Seeing them is making me upset, and I don't know if it's because I'm being hit by all the trauma that was interrupted by my walking in on Marshawn and Junior, or because I don't know how many of these people know I was there and will want to talk about it.

I freeze as Silas heads toward the front where the casket and immediate family are. "I'm gonna stay back here," I murmur. I can barely see straight right now.

"Shit, you okay?" Silas is empathetic. He leads me to the last row in the back, on the side opposite from the door where everyone comes in. "Just take it easy. I know it's a lot to deal with. I'll come back to check on you. Just take your time."

I fucking love Silas, man. I mean, you know what I mean.

Eleven diaphragmatic breaths later, I am twenty percent calmer when I look to my right and in walks Dinko, Nikki, and Sharmel, as if they all rode together. I look away from them and toward the front in hopes that they can't tell I'm on the verge of a panic attack. I forgot to add Nikki to my list of people who know I was there. Shit, she barely escaped being there. I can just give it up at this point and operate as if everyone—in the hood at least—already knows. Time to move to Plan B: *I am too traumatized to talk about it. I don't remember anything at all about that night. I must have blocked it out to cope.*

The three of them walk right toward me instead of toward the family up front. Sharmel enters the row first, then Nikki, then Dinko, carrying a box. While this gesture reminds me that I'm not alone in this trauma and secrecy, I realize how far removed I feel from them in such a short period of time. My new job, my better feeling about being at Marshawn's, my outlook on the near future, and my friendship with Silas have me feeling like a stranger to who I was two weeks ago. I didn't even spend a whole lot of time with their crew, but during the fun times I did have with them, I felt at home. Now, I feel different from them, like an outsider.

Dinko and Nikki nod their greetings, and Sharmel bursts into tears. I put my arm around her and hold on. Poor baby. I wonder where her family is during all this. I allow my own tears to fall silently. Silas is talking to friends but watching us.

Kai and Junior walk up to the end of our row and Dinko gets up to talk to them. He opens the box he is carrying and shows them the white t-shirts inside. On the front of the shirts is a picture of Bond in his signature blue fisherman hat, smiling and happy. Above the picture are the words "Rest In Power" and beneath the picture are the words "James Bond The Magnetic." When Dinko turns a shirt around to show the back, I see the phrase "Raise Your L Up In The Air For A Real One."

I'm admiring the lack of concern for the rules of capitalization when Bond's father starts hollering, "Get that dumb shit outta here! Get it outta here now!" He tries to rush toward Dinko, but his sons hold him back.

Bond's brothers shout, "Dad, stop!" and "Let it go!"

Dinko is crying, yelling, "I loved him too! Y'all ain't never believe in him! I did!" His friends take him and his box of shirts out of there.

Nikki got up, handed Sharmel a small pack of tissues, and followed them out. Meanwhile, Sharmel and I retreat again into one another's tears.

"They been fightin' like cats and dogs over there," Sharmel fretted when she took a break from crying. "They threatened to put Dinko out after he said one of them stole his weed. So while they arguin' about that, Mr. Bond blamed him for the shootin' like the shootin' was over weed or drugs."

Oops. I guess he did come back looking for that weed.

"I don't even go over there no more," she adds.

"I can't blame you," I say. "That's too stressful on top of everything else."

At a quarter to 6, Dinko, Nikki, Kai, and Junior return. They all sit on the back row with us. A few seconds later, the county's little delegation (including Selena) arrives with a police officer in uniform, two in suits, and a few folks from the town council (including Ms. Stave and the mayor). They are so focused on going up to greet the family that I can hide from them all very easily in my seat.

By the time Bond's father gets agitated and is asking, "When are y'all going to find who killed my son?!" the funeral has been opened to the public and dozens of people are pouring into the room, most lining up to view Bond's body in the casket.

Silas makes his way back and sits directly in front of me in the next row. I would have preferred to sit with him but staring at the tight curls in the back of his head is still comforting.

It's for the best that the program was limited to a eulogy and remarks from three family members, including one of his brothers. The place is packed, and looking at this crowd, somebody probably would have gotten a hold of the mic and started rapping.

When it's over and the people do a proper row-by-row exit, Silas hangs back so he can walk with me out of there. I am mentally preparing for the looks or questions we will get once outside, but outside is a new adventure entirely.

From a group of about twenty cars and fifty people in the far parking lot, Bond's popular song is blaring, and young people are shout-rapping the lyrics. Others from the public have moved closer to the people pouring out from the funeral home, as the casket is going into the hearse. A lot of them are wearing t-shirts different from Dinko's design to commemorate Bond and his music.

Bond's father softened upon seeing the outpouring of love from so many young people. He tearfully raises a hand to the fans close by and then to the ones in the far parking lot. They cheer loudly at his gesture, and I can hear calls of, "Rest in power, James Bond!" and "Raise a L for James Bond!"

I overhear Kai telling Gene that the family is only telling a few close friends where Bond will be buried because they don't want fans and news crews showing up. Then, Kai comes up and wraps his arm around my shoulders, which feels both loving and like a message to Silas.

As the crew I have come to know and love gathers—Kai, Silas, Junior, Gene, Dinko, Sharmel, and even Nikki—the familiar feeling of home looms just out of my reach.

About twenty feet away, I spot Selena waving to us.

"Who is that?" Gene marvels.

"Work shit," Silas replies.

"Introduce me!" Gene is always gonna be Gene.

Selena waves again.

Silas looks at me. "You okay to talk to work folks?"

I feel all of our crew's eyes on me. I am sure they all know I work for the County by now. I shrug and release the need to pretend that everything is okay. Besides, I'm on Plan B: traumatized and oblivious. My true mix of feelings works well for my pretend condition, and my face is stone.

"Why are all these officials here?" asks Nikki.

"They doin' a new community police thing," Silas answers, solemn. "I guess they had to start somewhere."

She cut Dinko a micro-look. He, too, has gone stone-faced. But I am watching him watch the county officials and the police.

I pat Kai's hand for him to release his grip. He lets me go, and Silas and I walk over to Selena. Once we are close enough to her, she leads us a few steps away to two men and a woman standing together.

"Silas, Ruhshawn, these are our contacts from the Prosecutor's Office and County Police." Selena says their names and we all shake hands, but I don't make a point to remember them. If my committee has to work with them, I'll see them soon enough.

"You two knew the young man?" one of the men inquires.

"From the same neighborhood," answers Silas.

"That's so unfortunate," another one offers.

There is more small talk, but I don't hear a word they are saying. I feel someone's eyes on me and am imagining that Dinko is wondering what side I'm on. It occurs to me that I am going to have to reassure him somehow. The thought of that is not nearly as exciting as it should be, as I am no longer willing to come up off hotel money to be alone with him.

The woman from the County Police looks over my shoulder and says, "Meet our trainer for the Community Liaison Unit…"

I turn around and almost pass the fuck out. "Sergeant Bradford Wallace."

22

Back in 1998, Bradford kept his word and got me a job working with one of his friends who was a private detective in Atlanta. It sounded more exciting than it turned out to be. I was the man's administrative assistant and did a lot of typing, filing, and organizing.

I worked there for six months, and then my boss got mad that I started a minor fling with one of the clients who was having his wife investigated. And then I had a minor fling with my boss' son. When he confronted me as if he was going to fire me, I quit. It was right on time, because I was already planning my move away from Atlanta when my lease was up.

Grandma, Marshawn's mother, had a mild stroke that October, so I was doing the family a favor by moving in with her. Marshawn had mixed feelings about it, though. On one hand, she didn't have to worry about supporting me financially or about paying a nurse to take care of Grandma. On the other hand, she didn't know how Grandma and I would get along.

We did Christmas at Grandma's house that year—that one and only time—and Marshawn and Thomas bought me a new computer with AOL installed so I could learn how to use the internet. Thomas was big into technology, and the gift came with a sermon about how I should go into computer programming because I would always have a job. That was another first-and-only that Christmas, Thomas saying more than ten words in a conversation.

Grandma wasn't that bad off, and I think she wanted some company more than caregiving. She and I were cool as long as my attention was solely on her. I got a job at a grocery store, working about 30 hours a week. It was good money for someone who didn't have to pay rent or a car note. I gave her money every month for her electric bill, and she always took the cash right out of my hand and went to spend it on something frivolous.

The problem came when I learned how to use AOL chat rooms and then Black Planet to meet guys. Wooo, chile, that was a *time*. Within a couple of months, I was going out several nights a week.

You know what Grandma had the nerve to tell me? "Your mother never stayed out all night in the streets." My mother was sneaking around with a man almost twice her age, that's why. Funny how she and Marshawn always try to play me like I'm the only young, single woman in the world who ever optimized my game and got dick when I wanted it.

I waited a whole year after moving in with her to have a guy come to the house to pick me up. She was so concerned about me "running the streets" that I wanted to show her I wasn't out running with crooks and robbers—like *she* was when she was my age. I chose the cleanest cut dude I knew to take me out for my birthday and had him meet Grandma first.

What I do that for? She asked dude, "Are you gonna marry her?"

He took me out for a real good time and never called me again.

At one point, I had three boyfriends in three different states. There was one in the state Grandma and I lived in, the state north of this one, and the state west of this one. By the time I narrowed down to one boyfriend in 2002, Grandma was done with me. She called my mother talkin' 'bout, "This child out here whorin'!"

I left her house and went to Auntie Zee's where I was appreciated.

Auntie Zee helped me get a job at a bank. I got me a cellphone right away, and then a new Honda Civic for my 25th birthday. Another benefit to living with Auntie Zee was that Kaia was once again close by. I had missed the way she balanced me out. She was my sister, no matter what.

She had finally loosened up a bit and was roommates with a girl she knew from college. Kai had an apartment in the same complex, and I got to see them both all the time. One of the nights she and I went out to a club, we met guys who would soon become our boyfriends. I used to think it was too bad that they weren't friends, but as it turns out, it was for the best that they did not have a connection outside of Kaia and me.

Kaia's man, Daniel, was an asshole. I peeped that from the first time we all hung out together. He was one of those people whose smile never looked genuine, and when he tried to fake one, he looked like a Cheshire cat.

I don't know what she ever saw in him. He had an apple head, average height, build, and intelligence, though he liked to believe he was smart. After some time spent around him, I saw his game. He knew Kaia was out of his league, so he made it his mission to destroy her self-esteem so he could have the upper hand.

The first time we went on a double date, it was to the movies and to get something to eat. He wouldn't let her get extra butter on the popcorn. I heard him tell her, "Unh unh, you gon' stop eatin' this kinda shit. That's why you got a double chin now."

So then at dinner, all she had was a salad.

I told Kaia that I heard what he said. She brushed it off and laughed like, "Girl, I do have a double chin! He's such a health nut. I asked him to help me do better." And then she looked me up and down and said, "*We* need to do better." As if I had asked her opinion on my weight.

He was always saying shit to her off to the side when he thought nobody else could hear him. One time, I heard him say, "See, you don't listen. You always doin' dumb shit." She just sucked her teeth, but she didn't defend herself or argue back.

I complained to Kaia all the time about him, but eventually she made it so there were no more double dates or wouldn't have us both around at the same time. I truly hated this dude, so that was cool with me, but then I started thinking of how bad it would get if she were truly isolated from people who loved her.

My next defense was to go to Kai about it. I told him, and he said that whenever he was around the guy, which was not often, the guy would be a perfect gentleman to Kaia and seemed cool enough to him. He also didn't want to interfere in Kaia's life.

What is it with people and this not wanting to interfere shit? That's the same thing Richardson, my boyfriend at the time, said whenever I complained to him about how Daniel treated Kaia. "Don't interfere. She a grown woman. She seems happy to me."

I had to take a different approach. I started acting like I was happy with Richardson and that I was happy that she was with Daniel. Eventually, Kaia was convinced enough to do double-dates with us again.

The truth was that I was bored with Richardson. In the two years we were together, we had actual penis-in-vagina sex maybe six times. During the first year, he kept me distracted with gifts, trips, fancy dinners, and fun. He was what people would call "a good guy" and he was nice-looking; he just wasn't into sex, I guess. But he never told me that. When I confronted him about it during our second year together, he blew up at me and said I was trying to emasculate him. Auntie Zee and Marshawn loved them some Richardson. Marshawn even insinuated that she was proud of me for accomplishing what I told her I wanted: a rich man to take care of me.

Unfortunately, after two years of Kaia putting up with his degrading, Daniel had gotten comfortable enough to start making his abusive comments out loud to embarrass her. The first few times he did it, they were both so used to it that they couldn't tell what it looked like to other people. When anyone acted shocked, Daniel would laugh and Kaia would say, "Keep playin' with me," or some other weak comeback.

But as her sister, I knew she didn't like that shit. And I was not going to let him break her all the way.

One night, Kaia invited Richardson and me over for dinner. She made lasagna, garlic bread, and potato salad. We were eating and Daniel said, "I'ma get my mother to show you how to make lasagna. My mother puts more cheese in hers."

I said to Kaia, "This lasagna is delicious!" I turned to him and asked, "What the hell is wrong with you?"

Kaia said, "Oh, please. Everything I cook, his mother's is better."

Daniel said, "It is."

I said, "So why don't you go fuck HER then?" It slipped out before I knew what I was saying, but at the same time, I realized why *m*therf*cker* is such a legendary and forbidden curse.

He jumped up and yelled, "BITCH! Who the fuck you talkin' to?"

I yelled back, "YOU! MUTHA! FUCKA!" And I said it like that to make sure he got the full curse. I wanted him dead at this point.

Richardson got up quickly and started pulling me toward the door as if I were in the wrong.

Daniel kept talking shit. "Fuck you, you fat ass bitch! Pillsbury dough ass bitch!"

Kaia found her voice then. "Daniel, stop! Calm down!"

Richardson found his only to tell me, "We leavin'. Get your shoes. Come on."

I heard Daniel say to Kaia, "I told your dumb ass about that bitch. See? You know she drunk too!"

I broke free from Richardson, ran the few steps

back to the dining table and hit Daniel in the face with the dress boot I had in my hand. Richardson dragged me away again and Kaia was trying to hold Daniel back.

He threw her off of him with the same force I would expect him to throw a man. She hit the wall and then the floor.

"Kaia, you don't need this shit!" I screamed. "What the fuck is wrong with you? Drop his bitch ass! What the fuck are you doing?"

Richardson threw my other boot out the door before dragging me out. When we got to his car, I didn't want to get in. I remember yelling about him not having my back and asking him if he was a bitch too. He drove me home to Auntie Zee's house but didn't walk me to the door. I told Auntie Zee about it shortly after I got home because she had expected me to spend the night at Richardson's.

The next morning, Marshawn called me and said Richardson told her what happened and that I was drunk and had provoked Daniel. How's that for a weak man? And she believed him! But of course, poor, troubled Ro needed to hang on to "the best man she ever gonna get," as I had heard her tell Auntie Zee once.

Later that day, Kaia called to apologize for Daniel and to smooth over the fact that he had thrown her against the wall.

I took a chance and drove over to Kai's apartment that evening. He was home alone watching a basketball documentary. Instead of stopping it when I came in, he gave me a beer and insisted that I hold whatever I was going to tell him until it was over. When the credits rolled, he used the remote to turn the television completely off, turned his body to face me, leaned back against his end of the couch, and said, "Alright. What happened?"

Kai is as handsome as Kaia is beautiful. Same honey-brown skin and eyes, thick hair, and attractive features. I had never paid attention to him like that because he was just Kai to me, and his older age put him in a different social circle when I was growing up. Seeing him as an attractive man for the first time threw me off, and I told the story in a much calmer way than I had planned to. His whole demeanor had defused me.

"A'ight, I'ma see him about it," Kai concluded. "Were all y'all drunk?"

"You are not listening to me," I said through clenched teeth. "Haven't I come to you before about this dude? And what does drunk have to do with it? He treats her like shit!"

"Like I said, he always been cool around me. But, I'ma see him about what happened last night." Kai's brow furrowed. "And how is *your* man doin'?"

"On his way out after last night. Weak ass didn't even have my back."

"I don't know where you be findin' these dudes, Ro. You gon' settle down one day."

"I can't have you, so I gotta keep looking until I find something close enough." I meant it. I mean, I hadn't been pining for him for years, but I definitely had him on a pedestal. I smiled at him, and his eyes didn't leave mine. He smiled back.

"You want me, huh?"

"Yeah. Why not?" I giggled.

"Come get me then." His tone was calm but playful.

I traversed time and space to jump on his suddenly sexy ass. Our kisses were so sweet, like we had real, genuine love for each other, like we knew each other and were safe with each other. We caressed each other, feeling familiar and carefree. It was beautiful.

My phone rang in my jacket pocket that was still on the other side of the couch where I had been sitting at first. I reached to turn it off, and in one smooth motion, Kai had me on my back, still kissing me. I found it anyway and turned it off without even looking at it.

When he took off my shirt, he said, "You want to?"

"Yes," I said. I probably giggled again.

When he got up to get a condom, I took off my pants and underwear. He came back, took off all of his clothes, and got back on top of me again. He was kissing and sucking all over my chest, then ripped the condom package open and put it on.

But for some reason, his dick would not go in. Like, I had to be wet, because I was enjoying every moment, and I know he was hard, because I saw it while he was putting the condom on. But we could not make it work. It was just awkward and baffling.

"Should I turn around?" I asked.

"Nah…" he said, confused.

"What the hell is happening?" I chuckled.

We both burst out laughing.

"Why, man?" he lamented between laughs. "Why can't we?"

"I don't know! I guess we're not supposed to?"

"Well, I ain't lettin' you up." He grabbed the remote from the coffee table and turned on the TV. We watched an entire episode of *Law & Order: Criminal Intent* naked together, with him on top of me. "I hate this fuckin' dude," Kai complained about Detective Goren. "They try to make him out to be so smart."

"I like him!" I laughed. "That's my favorite character."

He let me up to put on my clothes, and we watched a movie. I didn't leave his apartment until around 2am.

When I got back to Auntie Zee's house, Richardson was sitting outside in his car. He got out when he saw me. "I heard you! Who was it? Who were you with?" He was livid.

"I was at Kai's house," I replied calmly. "What'chu talkin' about?"

"You answered the phone, but you didn't hang up. I could tell you were fuckin' somebody!"

I am sure my face gave me away. But I had already decided I was done with Richardson, so I didn't care. "I did not fuck anybody. You better get from yelling in front o' Auntie Zee's house. You know she don't play that drama shit."

Auntie Zee was right on time opening the front door.

"Why the fuck you in front of my door with all this noise?" she asked through the screen. She didn't even raise her voice.

"She fuckin' somebody!" Richardson yelled.

"You know better than to bring this shit to *my* door." She still didn't raise her voice. "I'm 'bout to show you my glock if you don't take it somewhere else."

I was walking up the walkway to the house and didn't turn around to look back at him when I got to the porch.

"Ro!" Richardson called.

Auntie Zee opened the door to let me in and stepped outside. "Boy, what the fuck I just say?"

Richardson got in his car and drove away.

♪ ♪ ♪

Fast-forward three months and Kaia was still with Daniel. She and I mostly communicated through text messages, and a couple of times we rode together to see Marshawn. I sensed that she was being a little distant because bitch ass Richardson—Bitchardson—told her that I cheated on him with Kai. I denied it, of course, but I don't think she believed me.

On the way to Marshawn's house one time, she said that she was going to let her roommate know that she wouldn't be renewing their lease. She and Daniel were planning to move in together.

I was NOT having it. And so, I made an executive decision.

♪ ♪ ♪

Bradford and I had not been in consistent communication, but like most others fascinated by looking up old friends on the internet, we had found each other a few years prior and had each other's email addresses and phone numbers.

I sent an email to his personal account:
When will you have time for me?
He responded within thirty minutes:
Friday the 19th. [NAME OF HOTEL REDACTED], [HOTEL ADDRESS REDACTED].

And so, we began. Again.

♪ ♪ ♪

I kinda moved the timeline of events forward a bit so they could have a more immediate impact on what I needed from Bradford. Instead of telling him about Daniel's disrespectful incidents as they happened, months earlier, I described them as if they had just happened hours or days earlier. Sometimes, I acted like they were happening in real time, and I would send a text giving the details. This took a little over two months to build, and I made it look like Kaia was rushing things by moving in with him.

Anyway, it was November, two mornings after my 28th birthday. We were at a nice hotel in a nearby city in which we had never stayed before. He gave me a gold ankle bracelet and two charms to put on it, a gold letter R and a gold letter B. I recounted the big incident in which Daniel threw Kaia against the wall and called me a fat bitch. I didn't have to eliminate Richardson from the story; I merely referred to him as "this weak ass dude."

"I didn't want to tell you right away because I didn't want to ruin your mood for the weekend," I told Bradford.

I could tell he was running his tongue over his teeth as his wide lips contorted.

"I'm going to see his ass gone from this world," I promised. "Where do I hide the body?"

His expression instantly switched to very matter-of-fact, reminding me of back when he asked me how old I wanted him to be. "Storm drain." He named a certain park. "They always findin' bodies over there. Let's get some breakfast and get on the road."

♪♪♪

A week before Christmas 2005, I was wondering why Kaia had not returned my calls and texts for two days. I went to her apartment, but she wasn't there, so I called Kai.

"She is alive," Kai confirmed, "but Daniel is missin' in action."

"Oh, fuck a Daniel," I said.

"She's upset," he continued. "I got her with me. Now, I'ma have to really get in this dude's ass."

Kai took Kaia looking for Daniel, at his apartment and other places he frequented. They called a friend of his who hadn't seen him. No luck. Christmas came and went, and still, no sign of Daniel.

I was impressed at how quickly Bradford handled the situation. I had been expecting him to ask me more details about Daniel, like where he lives and where he goes. But I guess he didn't need my help.

I sent him a text.

I guess somebody storm drained his ass after all.

The new year started, and Kaia had not heard a

peep. That's when she finally said out loud that he may be dead.

In February, one of his friends called to give her the news. They found three bodies in the park Bradford mentioned—in the storm drain. Daniel's was one of them.

Bradford never replied to that text or to any others I sent to that number. He also didn't reply to any more of my emails. I eventually got a MAILER-DAEMON notice that my email was undeliverable.

My first fearful thought was that Bradford was also dead. He always responded to me within 24 hours. My second thought was that he had to stop communicating with me so that no one would link my texts and emails about Daniel back to him. It dawned on me that if those were discovered, he and I would both be suspects in Daniel's murder.

My mind went in a million different directions, and most of 2006 is a blur to me because I was in constant fear that the police would come looking for me for having Daniel killed. I was glad Kaia was finally safe from his abuse and I felt nothing at all about his ass being dead, but I didn't want to go to jail for it.

On one smoked out whim pondering 'If you didn't have much time left, what would you do?' I decided I should finish college.

While I was researching schools, I saw something that shined a ray of light into my dark cave. On the front page of an HBCU's website was Courtney's picture. My brilliant, little-dick activist professor Courtney from eleven years prior. They had a vivid shot of him talking with a group of students who were sitting on the steps outside of a campus building. Same ol' Courtney, but more mature and confident.

I clicked on it, and he was an Assistant Professor of Sociology. Whew.

23

Selena is frantically, unnecessarily, tucking her hair behind her ears. The bitch is beaming, she so damn thirsty.

Bradford is going gray, and it is so fucking sexy. His salt-and-pepper temples and close-cut beard are framing those pillow lips perfectly.

He shakes Silas' hand first. I think he is allowing me an extra second to compose myself.

"Sergeant Wallace," he says to me, shaking my hand limply and then going straight for Selena's hand without waiting for me to say my name. "Y'all camera-ready?" he asks in his standard cool and collected manner.

Selena, the prosecutors, and the other police people straighten up and start following Bradford away toward the news crews. Silas and I start walking back toward our neighborhood crew.

"Selena 'bout to throw it at dude," Silas chuckled. "Watch."

I'm, like, not even walking right now. I am supernaturally making my way across the parking lot because I am not really here. I don't know where I am.

We reach the crew as Kai is telling everyone that

he will be driving Dinko to the burial site. Dinko, however, is staring at my chest.

"Y'all wanna get something to eat?" Nikki asks.

Gene and Sharmel murmur about not having any money. I'm not trying to spend any money, and I say so.

"Let's all get up on Saturday," Junior offers. "Come to my house and we'll do something in the yard."

"Bet!" Gene says.

The rest of us nod and agree, then part ways. The public crowd has not thinned out because now folks are trying to get several seconds of fame on the news.

"You gon' be okay gettin' home?" Silas asks me.

"Yeah, I'll be alright."

I must have driven home by muscle memory because I don't remember the drive. Plopping on my bed, I am still in a daze.

Marshawn appeared at my door, which I hadn't bothered to close. "You okay?" she asks.

"Nope," I admit.

She comes into the room and takes my shoes off my feet before she sits on the bed. Damn, I forgot to take off my shoes?

"Did the funeral make it real? Being there when he got shot?"

"It's real, alright." I am muffled by my pillow. I wish I could tell her the whole Bradford story and how he just re-entered the picture, and how that makes me feel, or that I don't even know how I feel about it. "I just wanna go to work and get on with my life. I don't wanna be no witness to a murder."

"You didn't see anything, right?"

"No, I was out back. But I think the people who

did it were the people Bond and Dinko were fightin' with at the show."

"Fightin'? What show?"

I told her what went down after the local rapper showcase. "And then the night he got shot, Bond said somebody saw Dinko's work van after the fight. Dinko told him to shut up about it, though."

Talking out loud is helping me put pieces together. Life was so much simpler when I was only worried about Marshawn fucking Junior. I keep forgetting that Sharmel has to be going through it even worse than I am. She loved Bond, and she is lucky to be alive.

"So you were there for the fight and there for the shooting." The gears of her thoughts are grinding.

"Which may or may not have been retaliation for something Dinko and Bond did after the fight." I guess the less I know, the better.

"The less you know, the better," Marshawn remarks as if she can read my thoughts.

Except she can't read that Bradford is back.

"Are you hungry?" Marshawn asks. "Can you eat?"

"No." Not unless she got some Hostess CupCakes in there.

"Get some sleep." She gets up and goes out of the room, but still doesn't close my door. She comes back a few seconds later, sets something down on the bed, and leaves out, closing the door this time.

I turn over to see two chocolate cupcakes. Sometimes, Marshawn be lookin' out.

♪ ♪ ♪

A night's sleep helped a little bit, but I feel like a robot going through the motions at work today.

Selena is especially chipper. "Sooo," she corners me when I come back from the ladies' room. "Your presence is requested at dinner tonight."

"Why?" I am in no mood for her cheer or for any professional networking tonight.

"Remember Sergeant Wallace? The trainer for the new police unit?"

My blood goes either hot or cold. All I know is that I can suddenly feel it pounding in my veins.

"He invited me, the people you met yesterday, you, and Silas to dinner tonight. We're going to pay for it, of course. On the county's dime." She flips her hair over her shoulder.

I am too stunned to speak. I find my way toward the desk I have been using and sit down.

She follows me, still talking. "He heard that you and Silas knew the guy who got shot. The whole thing is turning out to be more high profile than we thought. There's some big-name rapper supposed to be coming to town for a memorial concert."

Bradford is pretending we don't know each other, but wants me to sit with him and other people at a dinner? It's always games with him.

Selena hasn't shut up yet. "With all of this attention, they are sure to catch whoever is responsible for the killing. I think he wants to reassure you and Silas. With the whole community liaison thing, you and Silas are kind of like liaisons in your own right."

My stomach churns.

"Are you okay?" she asks, realizing the look of actual pain on my face.

"I have to use the …" I get up and bolt out of there, back to the bathroom.

I make it to the toilet with my pants down just in time for my bowels to evacuate.

♪ ♪ ♪

Instead of going back to our office, I head toward Silas. When I get there, his office is dark and locked, so I go out the front door of the building and call him.

"Hello, I'm on my way back to the office right now." He rushes the statement as if he doesn't want me to start talking yet.

"Okay, see you then." I choose a bench outside and sit there, staring at nothing until I see Silas' car ten minutes later.

He must have seen me as he was driving in, because he walks out of the garage and comes to sit next to me on the bench. "You heard about dinner tonight?"

I nod.

"Look like this community liaison trainer tryna use Bond's murder as his jumping off point. I don't know how I feel about that."

I shake my head. "Well, I'm not sayin' shit. I am not gonna be their token community person."

Bradford wouldn't put me through that, would he?

"I'ma go," Silas says, "but just to see what they talkin' about. I do want them to catch who did it."

"Good idea," I conclude. "I been runnin' from

this shit. I mean, I don't want no parts of it, but I do want to know what they know."

My attachment to Silas is not strong enough for me to tell him that I was fucking Sergeant Wallace on and off for ten years or that he and I are bonded in ways that no one could ever understand.

"You wanna ride together?" Silas asks.

I love the way Silas takes care of business and takes care of me. But arriving to dinner with him will put too many thoughts into Bradford's head. And even though I used to like when he got jealous, I don't want to make Silas a target.

"Nah," I say. "Selena has already been asking too many questions."

He scoffs. "Good point."

♪ ♪ ♪

Selena gave me all the details before we left work for the day. She said she purposely scheduled dinner for 8pm so we would have time to "go home and change into our going out clothes."

I arrive ten minutes late because I didn't want to wait around awkwardly with everyone before being seated. Marshawn wasn't home when I left, but I borrowed one of her other old dresses that we had decided was too scandalous-side-chick for the funeral.

When I walk up to the table, I am partially relieved, first, that my old oyster-eating buddy Jones is here, and second, that Bradford is late. This makes me feel like I can collect myself before he arrives. However, Jones also acts as if he doesn't know me. I need to figure out if this is part of the professional game, or something I should be concerned about.

The round table seats five, and Jones is sitting between Silas and Selena. I would rather sit beside Silas than beside Selena, but either way, I'll be sitting beside Bradford. Selena eyes quickly dart from mine to the seat next to Silas. I take the cue that she wants to cozy up to Bradford. I oblige her and wonder why none of the others she named earlier are here.

Bradford arrives thirty seconds behind me. "My apologies, all. My first meeting with the unit ran late."

I guarantee you he was here 15 minutes early to see who arrived together.

"Councilman Jones," he greets, as Jones stands up to shake his hand.

Councilman? Yikes or yay?

"Miss Bell," he nods at me. "Mr. Mercer. Miss Benson." He nods to each as he sits down.

"Sorry the others couldn't make it," Selena apologizes.

"But I'm your consolation prize," Jones chuckles.

Selena and Jones order two bottles of wine and we peruse the menus. She is managing to project professional interest in Bradford rather than lustful thirst. *How long have you been doing these trainings? Do you have to tailor what you do to fit each police department?*

Bradford smells fucking delicious, though. Is that a hint of fruit on top of the cedarwood? The scent of his body chemistry has always been like kryptonite to me.

"That's a nice scent you have on," he comments to me.

What the hell? Is he reading my thoughts too?

He managed to keep it from sounding creepy or offensive. He even didn't attempt to make it a secret or say it under his breath. "What brand?" he asks.

What is he doing?

"She's not going to tell you," Selena interjects, leaning over to him so he can get a whiff of her too. "I asked her once and she said it was only soap and lotion."

Jones chimes in, "You know, that reminds me of my grandmother. She said the exact same thing! Talkin' 'bout a lady needs her own signature scent!"

Good lookin' out, Jones. He laughs good-naturedly and we all follow his lead.

Except Selena. "Yeah, an old lady would say that!"

"Hey, nothing like a classic, classy lady!" Bradford proclaims.

"Amen!" adds Silas.

I am blushing now, caught somewhere among feeling flattered and supported by the men, superior to Selena, and scared that Bradford and Silas are about to start sizing each other up.

The server brings the wine, disrupting the tension I'm feeling from Selena. After we order, Bradford initiates a conversation on local seafood, distribution, and specialties by geographic area. Silas' nerdy ass jumps right on into it. I hope I don't look as uncomfortable as I feel. You should see me trying to ration out my gulps of wine.

Bradford has further matured into his own brand of charming, having gone from lost-member-of-Wu-Tang cool to Denzel-Washington-as-Easy-Rawlins cool in his well-fitted charcoal suit. Unfortunately, still extremely fuckable. And this little game of flattering me, intentionally putting me above Selena, and pretending to be doing it as a stranger is … working on me.

Meanwhile, Silas keeps glancing at me to make sure I'm okay. If I am catching this, I know Bradford is.

"Can I get a Maker's Mark on the rocks?" Bradford asks the server.

"Make that two," pipes Selena.

Silas looks at me as if to see if I want one. Dammit. He's gotta stop being so obvious.

"I'm good, thanks." I need my wits about me as I pretend to be a classy professional who has not fucked the guy to my left or almost fucked the guy to my right.

Silas and Jones also decline the liquor. I see we all fakin' like vegan bacon up in here.

"Miss Bell, Mr. Mercer," Bradford began, "I wanted you to join us so I could personally reassure you that the county authorities are doing all they can to find and prosecute the person or persons who murdered James."

"Thank you," says Silas. "Do they have any leads yet?"

"Nothing as solid as they'd like," Bradford responds. "You know how it is. People ain't doin' much talkin'."

"Can you two ask around?" Selena asks, looking at me and Silas.

The rest of us share a microsecond of looking at her like she's stupid.

Bradford is nice about it. "That may not be the best course of action for James' particular community. We're also dealing with other young people who are fighting for their chance to be famous rappers. That brings a lot of other factors into play."

Fighting for their chance? Does he know about the fight after the showcase already?

"Yeah, I keep forgetting about the rapper thing," says Selena.

Jones shakes his head. "Young people today, dying to be the next instant celebrity."

I really liked Bond. He was happy and he was a good little dude. He wasn't flashy or dying to be a celebrity. He was ordinary and he still made an impact on his community, even with a simple, feel-good song.

"I'm so sorry, Ruhshawn," Selena offers, "I can tell it's upsetting for you."

Silas reaches for my hand and I jump. Just then, the server appears and shouts, "Lobster stuffed mushrooms!" and reaches between me and Silas to place the hot ceramic plate on the table.

He is really going to have to check himself on being so obviously attentive toward me. I don't think anyone caught that, and if they did, they aren't showing it. The rest of the dinner is jovial with very little work talk, thanks to Jones and Selena.

At 10:15pm, when we are all full, chilled-out, and wrapping it up, Bradford pulls out his business card and hands it to Silas. "I wanna keep the unit in touch with the business folks, man. Keep me in the loop."

"Will do, thank you," Silas agrees.

As we are all walking out the door and saying goodbyes, Bradford says, "I'm sorry, Miss Bell. I didn't mean to leave you out." He hands me his business card.

"Thank you," I say, and put the card in my purse without looking at it. "Good night."

When I get into my car, my phone rings immediately, and it's Silas. I can't help but be disappointed that it's not Bradford, but I can see him standing outside the restaurant being chatted up by Selena.

I answer Silas' call.

"You okay to drive home?" Silas asks.

"Yes, I only had two glasses."

"Hey, when you got upset, I wanted to hold your hand, you could probably tell, but then I remembered what you said about Selena asking questions."

"Right," I exhale. "But nah, I'm okay. Thanks for asking."

"What'chu waitin' for?" he asks.

"Huh?"

"Why you not drivin' off yet?"

"Because I answered your call!"

"You bein' nosey," he accuses. "I told you Selena was gon' throw it at dude."

I take it he didn't perceive the vibe between me and Bradford. Good.

I play it off with a laugh. "You caught me. Okay, I am driving away now. Okay?"

"Okay."

"Good night, Mr. Mercer."

"Good night, Miss Bell."

I pull out of the parking lot and Silas follows. Last I saw, Selena was still hair tossing and ear tucking, and Bradford was letting her.

I am not jealous.

At a stoplight, I reach into my purse and get Bradford's card. For some reason, I turn it over. There it is. Another phone number written in pen on the back.

I can't dial the number now that the light turned

green. Silas is still behind me, and we have a quarter of a mile before we get on the highway. But I know how to shake him off. When we get on the highway, I stay in the second lane from the right, keeping my speed at 60mph. It doesn't take long for him to ball out from behind me and speed past, honking his horn.

I pull off on the next exit, turn into a gas station, and call Bradford.

"There she is," he says upon answering.

"You finished talking to your girlfriend?" I demand.

"Woman, get your ass back here."

♪ ♪ ♪

When we get inside Bradford's small, temporary apartment, he shuts the door, locks it, and tosses his suit jacket onto the nearby couch. Before I can even look around, he grabs me, and hugs me tightly.

His arms are once again my medicine. His embrace is security. His touch is pure bliss. He is holding on to me as if I am providing the same for him.

We exhale, let go of the hug, and join hands instead. Our familiar feelings are still there as we stare into each other's eyes.

"Did you wear this dress for me?" he asks, staring at my cleavage.

I smirk and narrow my eyes. "No, but your girlfriend Selena wore *hers* for you."

"Hm. Too bad." He drops my hands and walks the few steps to the kitchen. It's a very small apartment.

"Can I get some water and a drink?" I take off my

heels. "I know you got somethin' to drink."

"You didn't wear that dress for me, and you want a drink?" He is already taking two glasses and some Grand Marnier from a cabinet.

Marshawn texts at 10:55.

>	Marshawn: Where are you?
>	Me: Afterparty. I'm ok. I won't be home til late.
>	Marshawn: Afterparty??

She so nosey. But I was in quite a state when she last saw me, so she may not know what to make of me not coming straight home from an 8pm dinner.

Shit, it's Friday night. She can call Junior after his massage class.

The first thing I do when we sit down on the couch is pick up his left hand to let him know I am looking for a ring.

"Yeah, that didn't work out," he says before sipping his drink and looking into my eyes.

I raise an eyebrow.

"I told you she wasn't you."

I took a big swig from my drink and set it down carefully on the small coffee table. I stood up and took my panties off. "Where's your bedroom, Sergeant?"

He set his drink down, stands up, and grabs me in one sweeping one motion. His kisses taste the same, and his tongue swirls mine the same. He starts walking me backward toward the bedroom and I can feel him bursting through his pants. I unbutton and unzip them. Once inside at the bed, he pushes me onto the bed and takes his pants and underwear off. Before I know it, he is on the bed and inside me. "You wore this dress for me?" he demands between kisses. He hasn't started stroking yet and I am getting wetter while he holds steady.

"Yes, just for you," I moan. He feels so good inside me, like he always did.

"I missed you so much," he whispers as he starts to grind.

"I missed you," I return, grabbing his muscular cheeks and pulling him deeper into me.

I am dizzy with desire and drunk off his scent and this big dick I missed so much. As I lift my hips to get the right rhythm for my first orgasm, I hear my dress rip. The evidence of our feverish passion turns us both on. I keep moving against him and come hard, yelling, "Brad! Brad!"

He rips the top of my dress with one hand and seizes my breast with his mouth. In a matter of seconds, he is climaxing. "I love you!" He can barely get out the words, "Tell me…"

"I love you," I say.

24

Brad and I found our classic rhythm again and again and again with intense sessions of lovemaking between catching each other up on our lives.

He kept his details limited, as he always did with police work stuff. I really didn't want to hear anything about the fiancée or whether she eventually became his wife. He wasn't wearing a ring the last time we were seeing each other, but I knew she was still around. Either way, they are done, and fate has brought him back to me. That is all that matters.

He got way more information out of me, asking me questions about how college went and what I plan to do next. I told him about everything except the university's assistant basketball coach who stole my heart for a while there. He seemed really excited about my current work and my plan to get a PhD.

"I'm proud o' you, Shawn," he says, slapping my bare butt as I am dozing off to sleep again.

The sun is coming up.

"Thank you," I answer, not even jolted fully awake by it.

"So. Silas Mercer," he begins.

Okay, now I'm awake. But I am facing away from him, so he didn't see my eyes fly wide open.

"Is he your boyfriend, or only tryna be?" His tone is not menacing. Not pathetic. He's asking the question as if he is packing up a fruit basket to send Silas as a *Thanks, but your services are no longer needed.*

I have to face him to answer so he knows that I am sincere. "Silas has become a good friend in these last couple of months. That's it."

"He likes you." He is searching my eyes for a reaction to that.

"I like him." I can't help my smile, but I feel that I am safe to be honest. Especially now that Bradford and I are expressing love for the first time in fifteen years. "But ... he's not you."

That slight smirk has always been his way of blushing. "Do you think we could make it work?" he asks. "Just me and you, picket fence and a dog?"

Okay, now I'm suspicious. "Why are you saying this now?"

"Why wouldn't I? We been through a lot." His eyes flashed. "A LOT. And who saw *this* shit coming?"

"This *is* crazy." I am trying to read his expression.

"Us being here together, right now, after all this time is crazy? Or what I'm asking you is crazy?"

"What are you asking me?" I can feel my forehead furrowing.

"I'm asking you if you can see us doin' life together."

Doing life together. What a strange way to put that, given that just four years ago I was scared we would both be doing life in prison.

This is what I wanted fifteen years ago, but even in those times we had when I was no longer so young and dumb, I just never got used to the idea that he could be fully mine. I have had to make myself okay with that. And now that I have lived so long being okay with him as a long-past dream, he wants this to be ... real?

"I have almost died twice at work."

"Oh my god, what?" I am sitting up fully now and turn so that my whole body is facing him.

"Remember when you worked at the drug store? I got shot?"

"And you got shot again?" What the hell? Did someone retaliate for that Daniel thing? "You never talk to me about your work," I remind him as I trace a scar on his abdomen.

He laughs at that. "I would rather focus on the good time." His face goes serious. "Nah, the other time was a head injury. A brain injury. That was worse that the gunshot wound."

"Brad!" I exclaim.

He brushes it off. "I like what I do now, but I want to retire soon."

"You old enough to retire?" I am thinking about Marshawn's workaholic ass talking about not retiring until she is 75.

He gives a dry smile. "Trust me, I got the years."

"Brad, how old are you?"

"Forty-three."

More than satisfied, I lay back down and go to sleep.

♪ ♪ ♪

Sharmel texted at 11am to ask me for a ride to Junior's house for the hood's repast. When I lean out of the bed to read her text, I see that Silas texted at 11:00 last night to see if I had made it home, and then texted again at 2am.

> Me to Silas: I am so sorry, I was asleep.
> Silas: I swear, now that I know you're not dead, I'm going to kill you.
> Me: Please don't say that. Not even as a joke.
> Silas: I apologize. Can I just choke the shit out of you for making me worry?
> Me: That's cool.
> Silas: See you at the cookout.

Oh, Silas.

Bradford picks up on my energy while I am texting. "I can tell you textin' your boyfriend."

"He's not my boyfriend."

Bradford's sideways frown is one of defeat. He goes into the kitchen and starts making us breakfast. This is a luxury I have never had with him.

Afterward, when I am full of eggs, sausage, and waffles, wondering out loud how to thank him properly, he declines.

"You never did answer my question," he noted.

My eyes drop as I begin to seriously consider what a real relationship with him would mean.

"Think about it," he said, getting up from the table and clearing our dishes.

♪ ♪ ♪

I could barely muster the energy to peel myself away from Bradford and mentally prepare to socialize and grieve with the crew. I probably wouldn't have gone if Sharmel hadn't asked for a ride.

Bradford gave me a t-shirt and basketball shorts to wear home, and Marshawn peeps this as soon as I walk in the door.

She narrows her eyes. "I know you didn't wear that to dinner last night."

"Nope." I don't want to have this conversation.

"I thought you and Silas were just friends?" Of course, she is probing.

"We are." Shit, I can either let her believe I'm fucking Silas or admit that Bradford and I are at it again.

"So where are your clothes from last night?"

"Where I left them." I pick up the high heels I just took off and walk to my room.

I fucking hate living here.

While I'm in the shower, I can hear shuffling and banging and a lot of back and forth in the back yard. I look out the bathroom window, and Junior and Gene are setting up a grill and tables. What in the entire hell?

When I get out of the shower, I wrap my towel around myself and walk to the kitchen to find Marshawn standing at the back door.

"They're doing it here?" I ask.

"Are we keepin' secrets or are we on a need-to-know basis?" she counters, unfazed.

I roll my eyes and turn around to go back to my room.

"You got a hickey," she taunts.

Fucking. Hate it. Here.

It takes me a few minutes to decide what to wear. I want to look nice, but we'll only be in the yard. My decision is made for me when I realize that all of my cute tops would show the hickey. I put on a t-shirt that I hope doesn't look too old and some stretchy jeans so that no one would be looking at the faded shirt anyway. The outfit is complete with my trusty black sandals that I am going to replace when I get my first paycheck.

Sharmel lives twenty minutes away. I complain to myself about the distance as I'm driving, but I'm mostly thinking about Bradford asking me if I could see us together.

When I imagine how I would break this to Marshawn, I think of her previous warning about how he may be after our money. But that was years ago. Is there even that much of it? If it is, I can't tell. I have to wait for a paycheck to buy new shoes, and we both have the same cars we bought a few years ago when I first went back to college. Like, seriously, what money?

I am surprised at how nice a neighborhood Sharmel's is. I don't know what I expected, but her neighborhood's median income is obviously higher than ours. This is the kind of neighborhood I would expect to be living in if we had all the money Marshawn claimed we did. When I pull up, she comes right out, wearing one of the t-shirts Dinko had at the funeral, and carrying another in her hand.

"I got you one, just in case Dinko gave them all away already," she says when she gets in.

"Aw, thank you." This is better than the Space

Camp Mentor shirt I have on. Yeah, fuck proper capitalization.

She fills me in on her life. I guess I thought she would live in a ghetto because she didn't have a car and I couldn't detect any family support with the Bond situation. Besides, she's so down-to-earth. She explains that her parents never approved of Bond or her friendships with people from our part of the county. Like me, she has always been a huge disappointment, and is living at home until she can move out again.

"Between me and you," she cautions, "Dinko is not doing too well. I called him a couple of times to check on him, but all he talked about was finding out who shot Bond and how to get them back. He's like, not his usual self."

"Did he do something after the fight?" I ask. "Like, before the shooting?"

"Probably." Her tone indicates that she doesn't know much about it. "He may talk to you about it." She glances at me. "He asked me if you were the type to talk to the police."

Like I said, I don't want to be nobody's damn witness. "I didn't see anything, though. I was out back with him, remember?"

"That's what I told him," she says softly, "but he in his own world. He been stayin' wit' Nikki though. And she kinda changed too."

I have never perceived more than bitterness, hostility, indifference, and general nihilism from Nikki. What could she possibly have changed into? I don't ask.

"Well, I don't remember anything. It's like I... blocked it out."

That's my story and I'm sticking to it.

"Me too," she admits. "But I wish I didn't. I want them to get whoever did it."

♪ ♪ ♪

The cookout turns out nicely. I cringe thinking about Marshawn and Junior planning together, but here we are. She even made the damn potato salad and is DJing from inside the house. She's making it easy on herself, though, by playing entire albums and 'Greatest Hits' or 'Best Of' compilations.

I'm sitting at a card table with Silas, Sharmel, and Kai. There is another card table where Dinko, Nikki, and two young guys are sitting. They look Bond's age. Two of Bond's brothers are at the picnic table with whom I presume to be their girlfriends, along with a couple of other people. Sitting in the random chairs all over the yard, there are about ten more people here that I never met and five I recognize from The Roost. Silas and Gene are doing a lot of standing, grilling, walking around, and mopping sweat with the hand towels flung over their shoulders.

Silas catches me daydreaming when Marshawn plays "Ain't Understanding Mellow" by Jerry Butler and Brenda Lee Eager. I thought of how easy it was for me to tell Bradford that I liked Silas without it having to be a big deal. ♪ *Didn't try to hide your love for this other guy.* How quickly I switched from thinking that I could end up with Silas some day, to contemplating how a life with Bradford would work. ♪ *There's a man who understands how hard it is.* Oddly enough, I feel like they both understand me. But while Bradford knows me for who I am, Silas has ideas of who I should be. ♪ *Wherever you go, you have but to call on me.*

"What'chu thinkin' about?" Silas inquires.

Kai is talking to someone, and Sharmel is doing something on her phone.

"Nothing," I answer.

"You got your arms all folded up and you not eatin'."

Just what I need, to be caught up between *two* damn detectives.

I pick up the hotdog on my plate that I didn't bother to get a bun for. I take a big bite and stare at him as I chew.

He stares back, unamused. "Really?"

With the last bite of my hotdog, I get up to go to the bathroom. All this damn investigative work Silas is doing on me, and he couldn't tell his wife was cheating? Sorry, that's mean. But I'm sayin' though, right?

The music has changed to Maze featuring Frankie Beverly. "Joy and Pain," indeed.

I look into the mirror as I wash my hands. Funny how I didn't even bother to put on mascara or lipstick. It may be my imagination, but I feel glowy from the inside, as if a night of continual orgasming has given me a boost. When I walk out the door, I run smack into Dinko.

"Hey!" I say cheerfully. I remember when having Dinko this close to my bedroom would have resulted in me pulling him in and closing the door.

"Lemme talk to you right quick," he slurs. He smells like cigarettes, weed, and no sleep. And it was him pulling me into my bedroom and closing the door. "You didn't say nothin to nobody did you?"

"No," I say. "Like what?"

"Anything. To anybody."

"Dinko, you were with me. I didn't see anything. There's nothin' to say."

"About the fight after the show?" he prods.

"Nothing," I insist, "I didn't see anything at any time. And I feel bad. I wish I could help, to find who did it."

"I know who did it," he confirms.

"Oh shit. Okay."

♪ *Remember when you first found love, how you felt so good.*

"Don't say shit because …" He is interrupted by Nikki bursting through the door.

"WHAT THE FUCK IS THIS?" she yells.

"Come on, Nik, I'm tryin to see what she know!" he says, keeping his voice down.

"Do you NOT know that's my man?" She takes a threatening step toward me. "Bitch, I am NOT the one you wanna play with."

"WHO THE FUCK YOU THREATENIN' IN MY GOTDAMN HOUSE?!" Marshawn appears behind Nikki. "YOU DON'T WANNA PLAY WIT' *ME*, LIL GIRL! GET THE FUCK OUTTA HERE!"

Marshawn steps aside for Nikki to pass, and Nikki backs up and says, "You got'cha mother here now …"

"WHAT?" Marshawn growls, pulling a baseball bat from somewhere.

Nikki walked fast out the front door. When she was safely down the walk, she turned back and hollers, "Keep his ass then! Nigga, don't come back to my house!"

Marshawn goes out on the porch to make sure Nikki keeps on walking.

♪ *Joy and pain ... are like sunshine and rain.*

Meanwhile, Dinko emphasizes, "Just don't say shit, a'ight?"

To make my point, I reiterate, "I ain't see shit, I don't remember shit, I don't know shit."

"Good," he says, then turns and walks out of the room.

♪ *Sometimes devotion ... and sometimes deceit ...*

As I follow him through the living room, Silas is standing there, and Marshawn is coming back inside. They both glare at Dinko as he walks by, but he just keeps on walking through to the back door.
"You alright?" Silas asks me, eyeing Marshawn's bat.

"I'm alright." I make eye contact with Marshawn and shake my head.

♪ *They're both one and the same ...*

"Let me guess, he asked if you talked to the police and told you not to say anything." She knew what was up.

I confirm her suspicions with a look, noticing that she made sure that Silas knows too. I guess she has accepted the un-truth that he and I are a thing now.

She puts her bat beside the doorframe. "Y'all go on back outside."

We walk back out and realize that no one else heard the ruckus that just occurred inside and out front. The repast guests are in a lively discussion about the rapper who has been announced for a memorial concert.

"It's gon' be a bunch of people who didn't even know Bond," one person complains.

"They know his music, though," counters Sharmel.

"Watch, they gon' give out VIP tickets to police and their kids 'n shit," Kai says. Folks murmur in agreement, and he adds, "What about his friends?"

♪ *Seems the things that turn you on turn you around...*

25

Marshawn

I called Thomas the day Roshawn came home from the funeral looking like she was in a state of shock. She doesn't know he is back yet because he is staying in the city. I told him that this Dinko may be trying to intimidate her and that I am not sure if she is someone of interest to the people that shot her friend.

But after Roshawn stayed out all night last Friday night, Thomas found out something else. Detective Bradford Wallace is back in town. At this point, I don't know whether she is fucking both him and Silas, or if the times I thought she was with Silas, she was actually with Wallace.

Now, do I let her know *I know* that Wallace is back? She hasn't exactly lied to me about it, but she doesn't correct me when I mention Silas either. I think that the less she knows, the better. As always.

Thomas' priority, I told him, was finding out if Roshawn is in any danger and then taking care of it if she is. The next order of business will be getting Wallace out of the way again.

26

The County was the primary sponsor (other than the alcoholic beverage company) of the James Bond Memorial Concert. Thanks to our friend Councilman Jones, twenty VIP tickets were reserved for Bond's family and friends. In addition to Bond's brothers, a few cousins, and two other young local rappers he was looking out for, Sharmel, Kai, Junior, Quiana and her girlfriend, and Gene received the passes I was given to distribute.

Silas worked together with businesses in the various districts to ensure that they got adequate advertising opportunities, and Bradford ensured that County Police publicly got the ball rolling on raising money for a youth performing arts program. Bradford also coordinated crime-solving efforts with police in the City because people had been talking about the fight that Dinko and Bond got into after that rapper showcase. I was the one who stressed the importance of the concert taking place in the County, so that any further efforts to "support" would drive money and resources to the County instead of to a nationally recognizable city.

Speaking of recognizable names, there is no way I'm telling you who the headlining rapper was.

Dinko was adamant in the beginning that it was all fake and he didn't want to go, but the day before the concert, I texted Kai, Junior, and Sharmel about the VIP perks, including a Meet & Greet with the rapper, free food, and an open bar in the VIP area. Next thing I knew, Kai hit me up to ask if there was any way I could get Dinko in. I had been holding a pass for him anyway because I was certain that his stage performer's ego would eventually take over. My hope was that having such an experience would turn his attention toward the spotlight and away from street vengeance.

The other catalyst for his cooperation was that Sharmel and I coordinated a social media scheme to suggest that the headliner perform a cover of "In Da Air" with Dinko as his hype man. It worked, and Dinko saw all the posts and reposts featuring a picture of him and Bond on stage that Sharmel took on the night of the showcase. The picture was also reposted by the headlining rapper saying he would be honored to have Dinko perform the song with him. So, Dinko actually ended up on the headliner's VIP list.

We all had a good time, but it is now an hour after the show, and some of us are going viral on the internet for different reasons, thanks to camera phones. First, Quiana and her girlfriend were very excited that they got to join the other young VIP pass holders hopping around on stage with Dinko and the headliner. Quiana's girlfriend got a little too happy and started doing some butt shaking, throwing it in a circle and whatnot, and Junior ran out there and snatched her ass backstage. He did it in one swift motion and it is pretty hilarious to watch on a loop.

Second, Selena took her thirsty ass out there with the young girls, and being that she was obviously well past jailbait age, the headliner was comfortable dancing freaky with her while Dinko rapped the third verse of "In Da Air." She was all off-beat, flat booty on the 1 and 3, flipping her hair like she didn't care. Half of the people posting the video of her know she looked ridiculous, but the other half are commenting on how pretty she is.

The third viral moment happened at the end of Dinko's performance. He started a freestyle that went off the rails into not even rhyming anymore, then into a rant ending at, "We comin' after whoever came for my cousin." Well, some smart person cut his mic, and the headliner—apparently an expert at maintaining control of a show—ended it with, "We thank law enforcement for catching the people who make it hard for us to gather in peace with one another. Rest in peace, James Bond!"

When Dinko started that shit on stage, I was stressed out all over again. After the concert, there was no shame in Bradford and I finding each other and leaving together. Hiding our relationship was the last thing on our minds. Silas had his older son with him, hanging out with other County people and their kids, so he hadn't been watching me like a hawk the whole time. But even if he had been, I needed Bradford.

♪♪♪

We are sitting on his couch, facing one another, rubbing each other's feet. I have to admit, spending time with him in the context of "I'm asking you if you can see us doing life together" has been pretty great. He seems more relaxed these days, but I guess being a consultant would give one more of a chill vibe than chasing drug dealers would.

Despite the fact that I started this off-and-on relationship in secrecy fifteen years ago, not seeing him for years at a time between escapades, I believe that I have always been in love with Bradford. Yet, I remain thankful that I have been able to grow into my own woman and that I have had other relationships and sexual experiences.

I would like to see what a real relationship with him would be like, out from the shadows, and respected by our family and friends. Marshawn has stopped her interrogation of my nights out, and I am less scared of revealing this relationship—under the right circumstances, that is. I am definitely too old to be doing this hiding shit.

Bradford has paused my foot massage several times to pick up his work phone, read the screen, frown, and type. This time, he picks up his phone and looks at me as if something just hits him. "Tell me again what happened the night James was shot."

What does he mean by 'tell me again' because I never gave him details in the first place? Now I have to think back on anything and everything I ever said about it.

"You're stalling," he notes, his voice steady and serious. "And you're scared."

"Why, what happened?" I ask. He already knows I am stalling and scared. I'll keep on stalling until I know what's up.

"Police are looking into a ... chubby girl in a red car."

Fuck.

And really? Chubby?

"Seen near the scene before and after the shooting," he continues, "and in another location with another person of interest."

Where else would someone have seen me in my car?

"You can expect detectives to question you at your house tomorrow."

"Fuck!" These tears welling up in my eyes are frustration on top of fear. Being afraid all by myself is one thing; bringing drama to Marshawn's house is another. She had a solid block of years without having to worry about my shit. I move in for one summer, and here we go again.

"What did you do?" he questions.

"I didn't do anything!" I protest. "I didn't even see anything!"

"Why are you scared then?" He is not showing any emotion.

"Brad, I don't want nobody lookin' for me! I didn't see shit!"

"Sounds like somebody saw *you* though." He doesn't believe me.

"Suppose they come looking for me?"

"Who?" he asks.

"Whoever thinks I know something!" I let the tears flow. So much for doing my best to match his cool.

I get up and pace.

"Roshawn." His voice is still steady. "Tell me

what happened. And don't leave out anything."

Well, if there's one thing I know, I know I can count on him to ride with me and for me. And in this case, I really didn't see or do anything. Fuck it.

I tell him everything, from the fight after the show, to the night of the shooting, to Dinko cornering me in my room. The only thing I leave out is that I had been trying to fuck Dinko before all that. Oh, and I didn't tell him that Dinko and/or Bond may have done something in between the fight and the shooting. No need to get Dinko hemmed up when I can't confirm any details about that part.

♪♪♪

Marshawn and I are sitting in silence. She is boiling mad. I am angry myself, but she is homicidal. The police just left.

Bradford and I agreed that I should be at Marshawn's house when they came. There was no need to have them looking around for me or to have Marshawn dealing with that alone. Of course, Brad's advice was that, based on my lack of information, it would be better for me to tell the police everything I know.

Right.

I came back here to Marshawn's last night so that I could wake up here. They came around 9:00am like they wanted to catch us before anyone would be dressed and out the door for Sunday errands.

When the two detectives walked in, Bradford was with them.

Marshawn's jaw was tight as shit when she saw

Bradford. Mine was too, but I was busy trying to pretend that we hadn't just spent two weeks as a full couple. He and the detectives were polite enough, though, and she was able to conduct herself as if she were okay with talking to the police.

After some pleasantries and basics, they got down to it. "We are looking into reports of a red car near the scene. Who is the owner of the 2007 Honda Accord?"

I said, "I am," at the same time Marshawn said, "She is."

"Where were you both on the night of Thursday, July 15th, when James Bond was shot?"

"Here," Marshawn answered. "And we live right around the corner, so that is near the scene."

"You were both here?" a detective asked.

"Yes," Marshawn affirmed.

The detective looked at me. "Was there anyone else here? Anyone else who knows that you were both here?"

"Our neighbor, Junior," Marshawn answered. "Excuse me, Foster. Foster Stave, Junior."

Marshawn's certainty that Junior would corroborate this alibi was a shock and a relief, but I didn't dare show emotion or look at Bradford's face. The detectives took down Junior's name and address. Then, they ceremoniously shut their notepads and looked to Bradford as if he were now in charge.

I just knew he was about to recount what I told him last night and blow that alibi up with dynamite. I braced for the impact.

"Ma'am," Bradford began, looking at Marshawn, "can you tell us the whereabouts of Thomas Swann?"

Another turn altogether.

And THAT—that ruffled Marshawn's feathers.

"He, uh … I don't …" It was clear to me that Marshawn has a secret or two about my stepfather, Thomas. Because she could have just told them he was out of town taking care of his mother, same as she told me.

"We understand he is your ex-husband, ma'am. We had to ask based on information gathered during an investigation. Are you aware that he is under investigation for fraud, ma'am?"

You get that? Her *ex*-husband.

"Fraud?" Marshawn seemed genuinely taken aback. Involvement in fraud is obviously not one of the secrets she was holding onto. She was chillin' when they were asking about a red car near the shooting. At the mention of fraud, though, I spotted the change in her composure.

"Ma'am, for your safety, please get in touch with your banking institutions, check the status of any investments, any properties. All of your financial dealings, we suggest you double-check all of it. We have reason to believe that Mr. Swann is attempting to use your name to defraud others."

Marshawn's leg started to bounce. She was holding onto Jesus' hand not getting up and tossing furniture around this place. "I would like more details on that, please," she requested in as even a tone as she could manage.

I was expecting her to tell me to leave the dining room and go to my room. But she didn't. They said they could only give her enough details to allow her to initiate the process of protecting her identity and checking with her bank. Because he has attempted to defraud people in several states, they said, Thomas' case will likely end up under federal jurisdiction. They also asked her not to attempt to contact him or see him, lest it appear that she was trying to warn him of his impending arrest.

She had warned me that Bradford was after our money, and it turned out to be Thomas. On one hand, a relief for me, on the other hand, a bomb dropped on her.

At first, I couldn't help but feel angry that Bradford kept this knowledge as police business and did not tell me before. However, I started thinking of how good it was that the police told Marshawn first, because I don't doubt that she would have killed him if she had discovered it on her own.

Between Bradford showing up with the detectives and Marshawn covering for me about where I was the night of the shooting, I feel a shift in loyalties rupturing what I had believed was a solid bond between Bradford and me. Like, it's me and my mother on this side of the law, versus he and his police gang on that side.

27
Marshawn

When the police left, my mind was racing. Is Thomas' fraudster ass better off dead or locked up? Yes, he deserves to die, and I hope he burns in hell, but maybe he would suffer more if he were locked up. I'm just not sure that fucking with my finances will get him the maximum-security hell I want for him.

What do you do when The Handler needs handling?

Now that Detective Bradford Wallace has done me a solid by warning me about this fool, I will speak to him directly about his relationship with Ro instead of having him forcibly removed from this area. Again. Especially since I don't know of any other way besides Thomas to get that done. For all I know, Wallace only came back and started dealing with Ro again to get close enough to help his gang catch Thomas. If that's the case, he'll be on his way out of town anyway as soon as Thomas is put away. So, that may just take care of itself.

My mother is the one who suggested Thomas in the first place, twelve years ago when I came to her about Ro and the Po-Po. Over the years, I have tried my best with her, but she really did blame me for my father's death and got downright nasty with me when the rumors circulated that both Roman and my father left me very well taken care of. With that kind of mother, who needs enemies?

Something tells me that this all begins and ends with her.

And I can be at her house in two hours.

My mother lives in a different house and place than where I grew up. Her home is modest and in a nice enough neighborhood, just like mine is, but even though she is the only one living there, she thinks it should be bigger. She reminds me of Roshawn in that way, wanting a bunch of big shit just to have it, but not respecting what it takes to maintain it. I am certain my father provided for her, but she was one of those women who didn't learn anything about how shit really works. She relied on my father to handle everything. I am sure that's the way he wanted it, but even so, why would he leave a lot of money to someone who wasn't used to it? Besides, her house is paid for, she has never driven a car, and I keep all her bills paid and more than enough money in her account.

When I get to her street, I park three houses down from hers so that I can walk up to her door without her being able to look outside, see my car, and possibly pretend she's not home. There is a Chrysler Sebring parked directly in front of her house, so one of her elderly friends may be over. She may even have an old man coming around at this point. No problem. I can sit here all day and bide my time.

Her screen door is not locked, so open it and knock on the interior door. Considering the unlocked screen and the car out front, I turn the door handle and walk right into the house.

Thomas jumps up from her sofa and reaches for a small black canvas backpack on the armchair, which is surely holding his piece. He recognizes me and slows his roll.

Well, well, well.

The police told me not to contact him, but here he is. I should have fucking known.

"Got damn, Marshawn!" he yells. "What—"

"What are *you* doing here?" I cut him off. I had to remember to smile, because I am not supposed to know about or confront him about his fraud shit.

"It's Sunday," he replies, still startled. "I came for dinner." He sits back down and closes the laptop that's on the coffee table.

It's only 1:00pm.

"You early, huh?" I pick up the heavy bag from the armchair and hand it to him before I sit down in it.

I remember when his six-foot-four-inch frame used to be all arms and legs. Now, he has put on weight, but it looks like a happy, comfortable weight, as if living away from our marriage lie has done him some good. His deep golden skin hasn't glowed like this since he first went to New York. At 58, he is still a very handsome man and fit enough that he doesn't look a day over 40. Still dying his hair, though. He is lucky that jet black is his natural color, but he will still look good when he lets it go gray.

"You think I'm not on my job, huh?" he asks,

smiling. "I am. And I'm teaching Mama how to use the computer."

"Tom?" my mother calls, coming down the steps into the living room. She frowns as soon as she sees me.

"Hello, Mother," I say casually.

"What'chu doin' here?" She is not happy to see me.

"You not happy to see me?"

She sucks her teeth and walks past me. "Did you invite her?" she asks Thomas, going into the kitchen.

"Yeah, Mama." Thomas rolls his eyes and crosses his legs. He lowers his voice and asks, "This is a little dangerous, isn't it?"

"Yes, and I'm sorry. There has been an update, and I would like to put that work on pause."

"Update?" His thick eyebrows draw toward their center.

"IT'S POLICE IN THE BACKYARD! THEY OUT BACK, TOM!" My mother is hollering and running into the living room.

Thomas and I both spring up. He looks at me with the question of whether this is my doing.

"No!" I answer.

The front door bursts open and Thomas reaches for his bag as I dive to the ground.

"DROP IT OR WE DROP YOU!" I hear as the door to the basement also flings open and boots make their way to Thomas.

"HANDS ON YOUR HEAD."

There is a knee in my back while someone puts cuffs on me. My mother is screaming as they do the same to her.

This is a lot for fraud. That can't be all this is about. But I guess I never knew all of what Thomas was about. I am lying with my cheek to the floor thinking of how shitty it would be to die here because of Thomas' activities. Meanwhile, they show their warrants for a search of the house and for Thomas' arrest.

28

Marshawn got home late Sunday night wearing an expression that I have never seen before. She no longer had the murderous look in her eyes, but it was replaced with the look of pushing away some other emotion.

She refused to talk about what happened when she left the house after Bradford and the detectives left, but she did mutter, "I'll tell you later," as she went up the steps to her room.

Something about her not going to work today told me something was wrong. She always goes to work unless she schedules a true vacation. And she never gets sick. Worrying about her has taken away my appetite. I came into work today anyway.

I haven't heard from, nor have I contacted Bradford since he left with the detectives yesterday. I don't even know if I want to talk to him. I guess that "doing life together" was a bunch of bullshit so he can solve a case. I mean, I guess, in the end, it's saving our money. But I was ready to say yes to him.

Back and forth like this. In my head. All day.

I am not taking my usual lunch hour, so I am in the office when Selena gets a delivery: a dozen roses and an arrangement of fruit and chocolates.

"For me?" she asks, tucking her hair behind her ears. "Oh my god." She shows the delivery guy where to sit the stuff on the edge of her desk.

Roy goes in and inquires, "So, who's it from?"

I don't budge from my seat. Fuck Selena. And that's just how I feel today.

I can hear her opening the card. She gasps loudly. "For a stellar woman and her stellar performance. I hope we can light up another stage sometime soon." She gasps again, then recites the initials of the rapper who bent her over on stage the other night.

You gotta be fucking kidding me.

While they are distracted and gushing, I text Silas.

Me: Are you busy?

He must be because it takes him half an hour to reply.

Silas: Apologies. I am in the middle of something. What do you need?
Me: Nothing. I was going to take a trip to your office to huff and puff for a few minutes.

Another half-hour goes by.

Silas: You want to meet for dinner at 6?
Me: Yes!

This time, a twenty-minute wait before he texts me the name of a restaurant.
And then at 3:30, Bradford calls.
And I do not answer.

♪ ♪ ♪

I left work early because Selena was gone by 3:48pm. Right after Bradford called me, she got a call on her office phone from someone confirming that she received the delivery and inviting her to meet up with the rapper. You know she will be some kind of unbearable around the office for the foreseeable future.

At 3:49, I decided I could drive home, check on my mother, and be back out the door by 5:30 to get to dinner at 6. Bradford calls again as soon as I get in my car. And I ignore him again. I just don't have anything to say to him right now.

Honestly, I would like my mother's advice before I resume my dealings with him. My, how things change.

When I park in my usual spot at the house and get out of my car, I hear tires screech to a halt beside my car. A medium-height, lanky individual dressed in a black ski mask, black t-shirt, and black skinny jeans jumps out of the passenger seat with a baseball bat and I haul ass toward the house.

I know I won't be able to unlock the front door and get in the house quickly enough, so I run straight to the backyard—thank God someone left the fence open—and hope there is a heavy object I can use to defend myself. I see an old, rusty shovel leaning up against the back of the house and I grab it and turn around, ready to swing.

I hear what sounds like glass being smashed out front, but so far, no one has chased me into the backyard. Immediately after the smashing sounds, I hear a loud crash, then what sounds like a struggling car engine, then someone yelling "GO! GO!" and then a car peeling away.

The noises put me in the same mindset as when Bond got shot. My legs feel so weak that I collapse on the steps that lead to the back door.

It sounds quiet out front for a few seconds, but then I hear the front screen door slam. Who was that? Someone heard that the police came to talk to us? Is whoever came to get us in the house? Were they linked up with whoever jumped out of the car?

I crawl up to the back door and lean on it so that whoever is in the house can't see me and if anyone comes to the backyard, I will see them before they see me. As soon as I think to call Bradford for help, I realize that I dropped my purse as I was running; it's somewhere between my car and the path to the back yard.

Five minutes later, I hear an engine that sounds like it could use a new muffler. It reminds me of how Junior's truck sounds coming down the street. Sure enough, it stops right out front. I hear a heavy door open and close, and I hear Marshawn's voice.

"I called her phone, but I don't know where she is."

I get up and walk slowly around to the front. My mother runs toward me when she sees me. She calls my name and puts her arms around me. I feel like I am watching all of this from outside myself. I think I am crying.

♩♪♪

"Our top story this evening: Two suspects are in custody in connection with the killing of a beloved local hero, James Bond. The 26-year-old rapper was killed last month in front of his home, a tragedy that warranted the joint efforts of City and County Police. Both departments say that tips have been pouring in, and without the help of concerned citizens, these arrests would not have been possible.

"Thirty-four-year-old Nicole Beane and 25-year-old Jamal Wakeland are charged with first-degree murder, witness intimidation, and vandalism, among other offenses. They were apprehended near the scene of the murder where they were spotted by an off-duty officer…"

♩♪♪

That day, Bradford had followed me from my job to the house after I didn't answer his calls. As he was creeping up on me, he saw the car pull up beside mine and the dude jump out with a bat. When I ran around back, the dude smashed Marshawn's and my back windshields. Before he could get back in the car, Bradford drove up and rear-ended the car, totaling his in the impact. The dude ran away, and the driver of the car struggled a bit to get it going again, kept driving, and then stalled out shortly after. The driver got out and tried to run but didn't get far because she fell. The chubby girl was driving a red 2006 Nissan Altima. Fucking Nikki.

Her accomplice rolled over on her under questioning. He told police that she gave Dinko and Bond money to get studio time, make mixtapes, and pay their way into opening for a bigger act. It seems she thought this would help her hold on to Dinko, who was cheating with different women and refused to move in with her. She was supposed to pay this Jamal to shoot and wound—not kill—Bond *and* Dinko. But dude messed up. At first she refused to pay him, but she needed his help again to fuck up me and Marshawn's cars. She promised him she would pay the original amount if he did this for her.

Poor Dinko. He left town yesterday, they say, to stay with another relative.

That whole ordeal was four days ago, and neither Marshawn nor I have left the house since.

Guess what else? The police didn't have any real evidence that Thomas was committing fraud with Marshawn's name. They told her all of that to get her to lead them to him. They believed that, even though they told her not to, she would still contact him or go see him.

Thomas is also being charged with murder, plus he has two attempted murder charges. One of the people he is accused of attempting to murder back in 1997 is Bradford.

Marshawn knew she couldn't pretend she didn't know about that. Not to me, anyway. It was too obvious. I bet she has been anxious to see whether Bradford would implicate her. I am confident that he won't, though. Our last conversation was Tuesday, when he told me everything.

Though the police made up the stuff about arresting Thomas for fraud, my mother discovered real evidence of his shadiness regarding her money. After Thomas was in custody for three whole days, Grandma sent my mother an email asking for her social security number to name her as a beneficiary for insurance. While Grandma thought she was only forwarding a form she wanted Marshawn to fill out, she was forwarding the whole email chain, including messages from Thomas telling her how to get at Marshawn's money.

Somewhere in those messages, Grandma mentioned Thomas' uncle, who was one of the men my grandfather enlisted to kill my father.

But I'm the family fuck-up, right?

Junior, Kai, and Auntie Zee have each dropped off food to us without hanging around to talk. Silas has offered, but I have told him that we're fine. We are not taking company, and we are barely speaking to each other. But for ten hours a day, we sit on the sofa together, taking turns picking movies to watch on tv.

29

My mother, my Auntie Zee, my sistergirl Kaia, and my new homie Sharmel are the first company I have at my new apartment. I make them a Sunday brunch for my official housewarming, served at my new dining room table, Ma's gift.

It's the weekend before my 33rd birthday, and we celebrate both occasions with Kaia's flavored mimosas and Sharmel's heavenly cheesecake.

After we toast to, "New beginnings!", "Love and friendship!", "Good luck with grad school applications!", and "Boss shit!" in that order, Ma hits us off with some news.

"I had a visitor yesterday," she begins, looking directly at me.

The rest of us sneak glances at each other and try to continue breathing normally.

"Sergeant Bradford Wallace came," she looked at Auntie Zee, "to apologize."

"For what?" Auntie Zee is not softening.

Kaia, Sharmel, and I, however, are metaphorically gagging in hopeless romanticism.

"Oh, for lots of things." Ma looks back at me, and

I'm back to being scared now. "But we had a nice, long talk. And we understand each other a lot better."

I bet both of their conspiracy-to-commit-murder asses do understand each other. Not to retrograde here, though, because Ma and I also understand each other a lot better now.

"Well, I haven't heard from him." I fold my arms across my chest.

"That's okay," says Marshawn. "You alright. And I'm alright. And we gon' *be* alright!"

"Cheers to THAT!" interjects Sharmel, and we all toast again.

It's been three months since Bradford and I have spoken. He is still helping the County Police get their community liaison unit together, and from what I understand, he will be here in that capacity for at least another month. Our work paths have not crossed since right after the funeral when he forced them to cross. I do miss him, though. I think about him all the time.

♪ ♪ ♪

Silas and I have been going out to dinner every Wednesday for a month now, but the Wednesday on which my birthday falls, I decide we should eat dinner at my place. He thinks it's ridiculous. We have been 'going Dutch' so far, and this time, he wants to treat for my birthday. I allow a compromise and let him bring dinner to me.

You're going to judge me, and I don't care, but for my birthday, I want sex. I knew a long time ago Silas was packing a punch, and I'm tryna get knocked the fuck out. We have waited long enough and have become good friends. It's time we get this sexual tension out of the way. Since everything went down, he has been less aggressive in being my personal security. My only worry, though, is that sex will put him back into bodyguard mode.

So much stress made me lose a few pounds, so I needed a new dress to provide the right impact. It took me three separate days of shopping after work to find something that fit just right. Without having to unbutton or unzip anything, I can step right into and out of this dress. It's a deep jewel-toned purple and perfect for being accidentally accessible when I pounce on him.

He takes his final sip of his second Jameson on the rocks, and it's time for me to see whether he is done for the night or doing me for the night. We don't even have to leave this sofa.

"If we get physical for one night," I propose, "do you think we could go back to normal?" I may as well let him know what I am thinking. A couple of mild traumas have weakened the filter between my brain and my mouth.

"Nope," he answers without the slightest hesitation.

"No?"

"I know what you doin' in that dress," he says, looking at me with no emotion. "It would have worked if I thought you really wanted me like that. If you wanted *me*, wanted to *be* with me. Not me for one night and then I gotta just be okay eventually seeing you with somebody else."

I am blushing. He's got me there.

"I never been the one-night type of dude," he declares. "Never."

Why wouldn't he let me decide later if I want him like that? Like, who does this? Makes a commitment before sex?

All I can say to that is, "But, it's my birthday."

At that, we both burst into laughter.

"So, what are you, like, saving yourself for marriage?" I tease.

"I ain't say all'at. But I would like to be monogamous."

I sigh. "I respect that."

"Hey," he reassures, grabbing my hand, "I love you. And because we are friends, I can tell you that as many times as I want to, and I won't expect anything from you."

"I love you too, Silas."

♪ ♪ ♪

Silas is gone already. Who leaves a girl alone at 9:30 on her birthday night?

Ciara is taunting me from the radio. ♪ *He love the way I riiiiide it.* That could be me right now.

I can't take it anymore. I reach for my phone to call Bradford.

And I see that he is calling me.

"Bradford." I answer immediately, but still don't want to sound as desperate as I feel.

"Happy Birthday." His voice is warm.

"Thank you."

"Your boyfriend left already?"

"WHAT?" I was about to fuss at him for violating my privacy when I hear a knock at the door.

I run to it and open it. He grabs me and hugs me, matching the desperation I was trying to hide.

After we hold each other for a few seconds, he pulls back and looks at me. "I'm not ready to let you go," he says.

"What changed your mind?" I raise a skeptical eyebrow, but I doubt that his answer will change my mind about inviting him to my bed in a few minutes.

"Changed my mind?" he asked, confused.

I would rather fuck first, talk later, but we may as well do this now. I break from him and walk to the sofa to sit.

He sits with me and takes my hand. "I asked you months ago if you could see us together, and it didn't seem like you liked that idea."

"I don't know," I confess. "Sometimes we seem so perfect together, and other times, we feel like we're on different planets. Sometimes, I feel like I could trust you with anything, and other times, I feel like you would put work before me."

"That's what we been dealin' with all these years," he points out. "That's the job. I do try to keep it separate from you. Sorry it had to go down like it did, but we okay now."

"Sorry it had to go down like it did?" I mock.

"I didn't know I would catch the people who killed your friend … or the dude who defrauded your mom … and who set me up to get shot. I mean, well, I had been working on that one …"

"You kept secrets from me," I protest. "And that

was after you left me in the lurch that other time. It's like we have a secret-secret that I would think kinda bonds us for life. I felt like you would really ride *with* me, ride *for* me. But all the secrets this time? I didn't feel like we were us anymore."

He looks confused. "Secret? Our relationship stopped being a secret for me a long time ago."

"No, the SECRET." I widen my eyes and give him an intense stare.

His eyes register nothing.

"Storm drain?" I remind him. "In the park?" I let go of his hand when he looks at me like I'm crazy.

"What are you talkin' about?"

I can't believe he is going to make me spell it out. "BRAD. When I told you about Kaia's boyfriend? Back in like 2005 or 6? Last time we were together for a few months? When I lived with my aunt?"

"Okay."

Wow, he is really good with secrets, or he really has no idea what I am talking about.

I lower my voice. "When I told you about Kaia's abusive boyfriend? I asked you where to hide his body. You told me where, and then they found him there. And *then*, you stopped returning my calls, texts, and emails. But I understood it then because—"

His eyebrows slowly unknitted. "Shawn, I got married on Christmas Eve, 2005. To prove to myself that I was fully committed, I cut off all communication with other women. Except family members and professional contacts."

Yuck, he *was* married, just like I thought.

"So you didn't put him in the storm drain?" I ask quietly.

He has the nerve to laugh. "No!" And he is still laughing. "What?!"

I stand up, take a step to start pacing, then turn quickly back around to face him. I am speechless. All these years, I thought...

"That's a nice dress," he says, tearing me out of my thoughts.

From the radio, I hear Ludacris rapping. ♪ *My chick bad, my chick hood.*

I put my hand on my hip. "Don't you dare rip this one."

He stands up, walks over to me, and pulls me to him. "Have you decided? Is it me and you doing life, or what?"

♪ *My chick bad, badder than yours.*

I smile at him. "I have decided that this is not how a marriage proposal is supposed to go."

THE END?

Acknowledgments

Thanks to Chris for listening to my ranting as this story went completely off the rails and for suggesting that I explore Roshawn's backstory. Bradford is your fault, just sayin'.
Mom, thank you so much for listening and laughing as I complained that the characters had rebelled and started doing their own thing. Thank you for reading my first draft and so enthusiastically bragging about this to family and friends.
Thanks to my sons for telling me that this book would be great. I hope you guys don't read this 'til you're 35.
Thanks, Kato, for giving me such thorough, invaluable feedback on the first draft. I can always count on you to go into the story.
Thank you to Nena, my kindred writing spirit, for giving me a fresh perspective on what this story brings.
Thanks to Tay and Rella, my SistaDocs, for reading early drafts, reacting as you were reading, and offering your promotional support.
Thanks to my mother-in-law and to my cousin Anita for not letting me blush too much about having you read this. I can't wait 'til your books are released!
Thank you to the many people who have been asking me for 22 years when my next book was coming out. Here ya go.